KILLER CRAVINGS

A MATERNAL INSTINCTS MYSTERY

DIANA ORGAIN

Killer Cravings

A Maternal Instincts Mystery

by
Diana Orgain

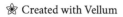 Created with Vellum

OTHER TITLES BY DIANA ORGAIN

CHAPTER 1

y stomach rumbled and my mouth watered.

Thoughts of jelly filled donuts danced in my head, only to be pushed aside by a chocolate-covered old-fashioned. No. A sprinkle-laden maple donut.

Ugh!

Stop.

I couldn't get these sugar-encrusted thoughts out of my head.

Cravings when I was pregnant with Laurie weren't particularly strong, but every once in a while, I'd go nuts for something; usually something salty. One night, I'd eaten two jumbo bags of pretzels for dinner, but that was about as far as it went when pregnant with her.

Pregnancy number two, however, was a totally different story.

Currently, I was sitting outside a small suburban home, my car parked with the lights out. I was supposed to be working a case, but all I could think about was getting something sweet. And, what made it worse, was that I couldn't quite figure out what sort of sweet I wanted. But, it was bad. Like, really bad. I couldn't concentrate to save my life.

My phone buzzed, so I put the light on dim to check it.

I am undercover, after all.

1

It was a text from Kenny, our next-door neighbor teenager turned nanny. I laughed out loud to see a picture of Laurie fast asleep in her crib with her finger up her nose. She was six months old now.

Six months old, and I'm pregnant all over again.

This pregnancy wasn't exactly planned, and the mind-boggling fact that we were having another baby before Laurie was even old enough to walk put me into full panic-mode. Even so, Jim and I were ecstatic. Nervous, but glad.

"Thanks for getting her to bed! Jim should be home soon," I said into the voice dictation on the phone as I texted him back.

Kenny is on the night shift because Jim had an out-of-town meeting he'd had to attend. He'd been gone for a couple of days, and I couldn't wait to see him. His flight was delayed into the dead hours, so he was just getting in. He'd texted me a few minutes ago from the airport, said he was stuck there dealing with a lost luggage issue.

Poor Jim.

Stakeouts look way more interesting in the movies. Something exciting always happened, but real life hardly ever behaves the way it does in the movies. I've been sitting in that car for four hours. Not moving. Just sitting here with my fancy new camera in the passenger seat waiting.

And waiting… and waiting… and waiting.

I was about to go insane. And, how dumb of me not to pack snacks? I knew I was pregnant. Why didn't I bring food? All I could think about was getting something sweet – a brownie, maybe? Ice cream? No, definitely a brownie.

I tapped on the steering wheel. When was this guy planning on leaving this woman's house? This was a new case given to me by Galigani, my boss and mom's current fling. A cheating husband case, and frankly, it made me sick. But, this is the sort of thing you deal with when you become a PI. Galigani got a lot of cases like this, so he felt it was time to turn one over to me. The woman was gearing up already, hiring a lawyer for the divorce, but she needed to bust him cheating. She hadn't been able to do it herself, so she had called in the A-team with Galigani, but with me it was more like the B-team, I guess.

There is a twenty-four hour doughnut shop about twenty minutes from here, I thought to myself, but I shook the thought away. *You have one job, Kate,* I told myself. *Get the picture, and then you can go home.*

Seriously – how late does this guy think he can stay over at another woman's house without his wife noticing? It's three in the morning. Surely he doesn't believe he can keep getting away with this? I think about Jim. I'm so glad I don't have to worry about this sort of thing with him. He's been loyal and dedicated to our marriage since day one. He's never given me even the slightest reason to worry, and for that I am really thankful. He's been amazing during this pregnancy just as he'd been when I was pregnant with Laurie. If anything, I feel like he does too much for me. Letting me quit my job to pursue training as a PI is just one of the many ways Jim recently showed me how much he cares.

Plus, he's an amazing father.

Food.

No matter how far my brain drifts off to something else, I always come back to food. I swear, it was never this bad with Laurie.

I pressed my hands to my belly. "Why are you always so hungry, baby?" I asked. Of course, I didn't get an answer with the exception of my craving increasing exponentially.

That's it. I'm doing it.

I started the engine and pulled the car out of the parking spot. The doughnut shop seemed too big a risk, but I knew there was a service station a few blocks away. I couldn't help myself. I needed something bad.

Like really, really bad.

I parked at the gas station and ran inside. The man behind the counter barely glanced up from his phone screen to nod at me. I dashed into the restroom.

Heck, may as well kill two birds with one stone.

Then, I grabbed a ridiculous amount of candies and sweets, checked out, and headed back. On the way there, I stuffed my face full of Reese's Pieces, but that was definitely not what I was wanting. Ugh!

I turned onto the street, and watched in horror as a man darted across the road.

Oh no...

It was him! He had a lumberjack build, a heavy black beard and even wore a red flannel overcoat.

There was no mistaking him.

I'd missed him leaving the woman's house! I pulled over, turned off my lights, and snapped several pictures, but I had a horrible weight in my stomach.

And not just from the candy!

I'd missed it! The moment I'd waited five hours for, gone faster than a sugar crash.

This creep hid out in her house all night, and I took a five-minute break to run to a gas station, and that's when he decided to leave!

Anger burned through my chest. Honestly, I wanted to confront him right there, slap him in the face, like in the movies. But that wasn't my job. My job was to bust him leaving the woman's house, and now all I had was a picture of him sitting in his car.

Real incriminating, Kate.

I'd wasted my entire evening all because of a pregnancy craving. Now, I was going to have to do it all over again. If I even had the chance!

Unbelievable!

I drove home, munching on a Snickers bar that made me nauseous to the point I had to pull over. Okay, it wasn't candy I wanted.

A warm feeling overcame me as I saw Jim's car parked outside our house. It was good knowing that he was home.

No doubt he was probably asleep by now if Laurie was in her crib still. I headed inside, depositing the candy and powdered doughnuts I'd bought at the gas station and began rummaging through the pantry. It was like a curse – some secret craving I couldn't quite figure out, and everything else was making me sick.

What is it that I want?

I think I tried four different treats before I noticed the sun peeking up outside.

You've got to be kidding me!

It wasn't fair! How did I manage to waste so much time on this stupid craving, along with ruining my stakeout. And, now I was being rewarded with no sleep.

"Kate?" a gruffly voice behind me said.

I spun around to see Jim wandering into the kitchen, followed by our orange tabby kitten, Whiskers.

My heart lurched to see Jim. "I'm sorry, babe, did I wake you up?" I asked, hurrying over to give him a big hug. "I missed you so much. Almost three days," I exclaimed, showering his face with kisses.

"Yeah, what are you doing? Did you ever get to bed last night?" he asked me, yawning.

"No," I said, my shoulders slumping from tiredness. "And, I screwed up the stakeout last night too!"

Tears welled up in my eyes, and I covered them with my hands.

"I feel like crying – call it the hormones," I said.

Jim put his hands on my shoulders and squeezed. "Aw, honey. Don't cry. What can I do? Did something happen?"

I spun around, pulling my hair to one side, to let Jim massage my shoulders. "You promise not to laugh?"

"I promise," he said, moving his hands from my shoulders to the back of my neck.

"I got this really bad craving, and I didn't bring any food. I left, and when I came back the guy was already in his car!" I said.

Jim laughed, so I whirled around and buried my head in his chest. "You promised not to laugh at me!"

He stroked my hair. "I'm sorry, Kate, but... it is kind of funny," he said.

"I know," I admitted. "But, this means I'm going to have to do the stake out all over again."

"Don't worry, you'll get him," Jim said. "How about the food craving? Did you get anything yummy? Did you at least bring me back something?" He rubbed his infuriating flat stomach. No matter how much food he put away, it seemed like he had a hollow leg!

At the word, *food*, Whiskers circled my legs and rubbed her cheek against my ankles.

"No! And, that's the problem. I know I want something sweet, but I can't figure out what it is," I explained. "And, it's driving me nuts! Look at all that junk food I bought at a gas station last night, and it all made me sick!"

The cat meowed.

"Did you feed her?" I asked.

"Yes, but she's always hungry too," Jim told me, and he went for his jacket that was thrown over the backs of one of our kitchen chairs. "I know what you want. You don't have to beat around the bush. You want a brownie from that bakery – the one with the purple icing, right?"

Yes! Oh my goodness, I'd completely forgotten about that brownie. When I'd first found out I was pregnant, I think I ate twenty of those things.

My face lit up, and Jim laughed at me. "Yeah, that was probably it. I knew I was thinking about a brownie. Wait, where are you going?"

"The bakery opens early on Thursdays," he said. "I'll go nab you one and be back in time to get ready for work."

"Jim! Don't do that," I said, feeling guilty. "You were up late last night too! And, you had to deal with all that nonsense at the airport."

"Do you want the brownie?" he asked.

I nodded. "Well, yeah, but I can—"

"Go lay down, and when I get back I'll wake you up, and I promise to have your special purple icing brownie, okay?" He pointed toward the nursery. "Plus, Laurie has been asleep since three this morning. Knowing her, she'll be up really soon. Go rest."

I gave him a big kiss before going and plopping down in bed. The kitten followed me and curled up on a corner of my pillow. I was exhausted, so sleep came to me easily. Painfully easily. The next thing I knew, I woke up to the sound of Laurie fussing on the baby monitor. I sat up slowly, rubbing my eyes because the sun was shining brightly through the blinds.

What time is it?

I hurried to get Laurie. She'd pulled herself up and was standing, holding onto the side of the crib.

"Good morning, gorgeous!" I said, picking her up. "You're becoming quite a climber."

Ordinarily, she couldn't stand, but with the aid of a support like the crib rails, she was a dynamo.

I changed her diaper and then sat and breastfed her in the corner, but she didn't seem interested.

"I know, I bet you want some bananas!" I said, and she cooed.

She definitely knew what that meant. I'd started mashing up bananas for her recently, and now it was her favorite snack.

I headed into the kitchen where I spied a clock. Noon! Laurie had been asleep since three... nine hours!

My baby slept nine hours!

I could hardly believe it. I sat her in her high chair.

Why hadn't Jim woken me?

As I opened my refrigerator, I found my answer. I found a plate full of chocolate brownies with purple icing sitting in the fridge with a note. It read, "You looked too peaceful. I hope Laurie let you sleep for a bit! There are plenty of brownies, and I went ahead and made Laurie some mashed bananas for you! Love you, see you later tonight! ~ Jim"

My hero.

I located the mashed bananas, and brought them over to Laurie. Deciding I was probably going to give her a bath shortly afterwards, I let her mash her fingers into the banana mush and feed herself. She had a good old time with that, and it allowed me a moment to pour myself a giant glass of milk. I then grabbed one of the very large ooey-gooey brownies and placed it on a plate for myself and sat down next to Laurie as she continued making a mess in her highchair.

I took one bite of that rich brownie with the light, fluffy purple icing, and I was in heaven. That was exactly what I'd been craving. I'd been craving that stupid brownie for probably three days. It'd been about a week since Jim had brought home some of those brownies when he had stopped by that new bakery, and I'd just loved them.

I'd completely forgotten about them, though. But, I guess the baby hadn't. The baby wanted that brownie so bad, and Jim had delivered an entire tray full in the fridge. The brownie was just so perfectly rich and moist even after sitting in the fridge for what had to be several hours. It was just wonderful, and I took my time eating it – enjoying every bite as it went down like it would be my last.

"Your daddy is so sweet, you know that?" I said to Laurie, and she giggled. Oh my goodness, just thinking about that brownie makes my toes curl a little. "Your daddy is just awesome!" I said just to make sure she knew.

I suppose that tracking down a sleazy cheater for a week could make anyone look good, but Jim was already exceptional. He was the perfect husband. He always looked out for me in ways I could hardly reciprocate. I felt truly lucky.

As I was daydreaming about my darling husband, I received a face full of banana goo.

Laurie was going through a throwing phase.

"No, ma'am!" I said to her, but I couldn't help but laugh as I wiped my face. I downed my glass of milk and then got Laurie out of her highchair. I brushed her honey-colored locks out of her face and tickled her chin. She had a full head of hair now; she had been balding a little bit recently, but it had all grown back just perfectly.

I carried her back to the bathroom, our kitten racing down the hallway to follow us. With my free hand, I ran some water in the tub, and Whiskers tore off and hid.

I laughed. "No bath, kitty?"

Laurie wiggled happily at the word, *kitty*, and looked around the bathroom frantically for the now disappeared cat.

Laurie still had to sit in her little baby tub, but I usually just sat the baby tub down in the bath to make it easier on myself. I took off her clothes, and after checking the temperature of the water, I sat her in it.

She giggled and squealed, practically screaming. She had this eardrum-piercing squeal that sounded almost like a dinosaur from *Jurassic Park*, but it was adorable in its own little way.

Jim would call it her *Pterodactyl yelp*. She always did it when she got really excited, and that was pretty much every single time I put her in the bath tub. We'd just gotten past a phase where she couldn't stand the bath, but now it was one of her favorite things. That and bananas.

Eventually the water got cold, and my little girl was clean. That didn't mean she was ready to get out of the bath tub, of course. Finally, though, I was able to coax her out, get her dried off, and dressed and ready to go for the day. I sat her down in her playpen while I got myself ready, and I could hear her quietly playing by herself in the living room while I ran back to the bedroom to get dressed. I was really starting to get the hang of this whole mom thing. Whenever things were going well with Laurie, I would get a new boost of confidence about being a mom all over again.

When I had first found out I was pregnant, it had been pretty scary. Another baby so soon? It seemed like utter madness. Plus, I had just changed career fields, making the news all the more insane. But, I was happy and eager to meet the latest member of my family now.

Once I was dressed, I decided to treat myself to one more rich, purple icing brownie before really getting going on my day.

And, boy, was it good.

CHAPTER 2

*N*ow that I was refreshed and ready to get going on my day, I decided I needed to write up a to-do list, and it was a mile long.

To Do:

1. Call Galigani, fess up about missing the photo op
2. Get a photo of the creepy cheater leaving his gf's place
3. Clean the kitchen because, ew
4. Pre-make tomorrow's baby food
5. Call mom
6. Ask Kenny to watch Laurie tonight
7. Get snacks together for stakeout 2.0

And, that was just the beginning. I continued writing down what all I had to do, and I started to grow discontent. There was no way I was going to get it all done in one day, so I just put a star next to some of the more urgent items.

As I studied my ever growing list my phone buzzed.

I grabbed it and saw that I had a text message from my best friend, Paula. *Must meet for lunch – have exciting news!!!!* I knew it must be truly exciting because Paula rarely used one exclamation point in her texts let alone four.

"Sweet," I said, but then frowned. I'd been having so many aversions to... everything. It was so strange. I hadn't had this problem with Laurie at all, but now I had to really watch what I ate. "Sounds good," I spoke as I typed the words. "Where?"

Lol – what can you eat?!?! Mexican?

Even more exclamation points.

She must be really eager to talk to me about something, I thought, smirking.

Definitely not Mexican," I said as I typed.

Chinese?

"Nope."

That sub shop down the street from the salon?

"Yikes. Last time I threw up in their bathroom sink!" I typed, shaking my head. The next text message came in.

You pick where, preggers.

I laughed and thought about my options for a moment. Food was the biggest challenge of this pregnancy thus far. That and the carbon monoxide poisoning I'd experienced last month. But that had been a mild scare, and the baby and I were being monitored for potential side effects

Food, however, was an every hour need!

I held the phone at the ready to respond, but I couldn't decide what kind of food I wanted.

I was pretty sure I'd already had my sweet fix for the day, and then I recalled a really awesome café that served the best baked chicken and mushrooms – and suddenly, that new craving hit me like a ton of bricks.

"City Café, please!" I texted her, and she replied with a smiley face emoji.

"Meet me in 30 minutes," she texted.

I was already dressed and pretty much ready to go, but I needed to get Laurie out of her comfy house clothes and into something worthy of *City Café*. The café had fancy French decor, so it wasn't really a sweatpants kind of place.

Although, my little girl was totally rocking those fluffy pink sweatpants. I changed her into an outfit my mom had recently bought her: a cutsie spring green dress and matching bow, complete with white stockings and little pink flats. It was so cute it was almost painful. I snapped a picture of her and sent it to both my mom and Jim.

Somehow, I managed to get Laurie into her carrier in record time, and before long, I was out the door.

Once outside, I spotted our neighbor/nanny, Kenny, out in his front yard. He was a seventeen-year-old musical prodigy, but today he was a regular teenager hanging out in his front yard, sitting in an Adirondack chair, ogling a blonde woman rushing down the street.

Kenny spotted Laurie and me and picked up his trombone and blasted out an excited tune that Laurie matched with a squeal.

He laughed, then ran a hand through his spiky, today dyed pink hair, and graced us with a wave.

Laurie kicked her feet in delight and strained in my arms to reach him.

"My goodness, she's excited to see you," I said, trying not to be offended by how happy he made her.

"How'd it go last night? Did you get your guy?" he asked.

I grunted. "Unfortunately, no. I missed the shot," I said, and he shook his head and tried to hide his smile.

"Shut up," I said.

Kenny laughed openly. "Do you need some help on the stakeout?"

"You are not allowed to go with me. You're more of a distraction than a help," I teased.

Laurie's hand hooked onto Kenny's shirt, and she pulled at him, screeching to be held. He offered her his hand, and she wrapped her fingers around it and yanked.

"Look at your pretty dress, little girl," Kenny said. He turned to me and said, "I can watch this Laurie, no problem. She looks like a little dolly in this dress."

"Thanks, Kenny," I said, just as a svelte woman jogger in flashy yoga pants turned our corner. Kenny immediately became distracted and took the opportunity to hightail it out of there. "See you later," I said, unlocking my car.

I hooked the carrier into the car seat; I loved the convenience of that thing. And, just like that, I was ready to go. I pulled out of the driveway, only having to turn back around before getting out of the neighborhood because I had left the diaper bag on the curb.

Kenny was standing in my driveway holding the bag, already pulling out his phone to call me, by the time I pulled back up.

I laughed at myself, rolling down the window as Kenny passed the bag to me. "Thanks," I said. "I have pregnancy brain really bad this time around."

"Must be a boy," Kenny said.

"What do you mean?" I asked.

"I don't know. You weren't that way with Laurie. My mom always said she had a harder time with me while she was pregnant than with my older sister. And, my aunt always said the same thing about my cousins too. I just figured it's one of those old wives' tales, but if that baby you're carrying turns out to be a boy, I'll believe it. And you puked in my mom's flower garden the other day, remember? I don't recall you ever having such a hard time with Laurie."

"That's true," I said, tucking the diaper bag away in my passenger seat. "Well, it's too early to know the sex just yet, but I'll let you know if your old wives' tale proves true this time around."

Kenny waved goodbye to me, chuckling at me for leaving the diaper bag in my driveway. On my way to the café, I set my Bluetooth to call Galigani. I wasn't looking forward to this conversation in the slightest. Honestly, I was hoping he wouldn't answer so that I could just leave a voicemail.

No such luck.

"Kate!" he boomed into the phone. "How did your sleuthing go last night? Did you get our money shot?"

There was no way I was going to tell him exactly what happened. Even though Galigani was a friend, he was still my boss, and I couldn't have him thinking the pregnancy was making me incompetent. "I didn't get the shot," I said, disappointment rattling my voice.

"Don't worry. It's not easy," Galigani said. "What happened? Did the guy ever show?"

"He did," I said, sighing. "Uh... I... I screwed up. I'm so sorry."

He let out a deep breath. "Well, no problem. Not yet, at least. Our client is leaving town for a couple of days to visit her mother. With that sort of freedom, we're bound to bust the guy hanging out with his side chick. He'll feel like there's no way he'll get caught with his wife out of town, so you're bound to get the shot this time."

"Good," I said. "I plan on doing another stakeout tonight."

"Way to be dedicated," he said. "Just keep me posted. You're still new at this, Kate. Don't beat yourself up too much."

"Thanks," I said before we both hung up the phone.

I was still pretty upset with myself for screwing up the way I had.

I can't let this pregnancy get the better of me!

When I'd been pregnant with Laurie, I'd felt like Superwoman. It had been such an easy-going pregnancy – a few hiccups along the way, of course, but nothing like this.

I need to be better prepared!

My goody bag for that night was going to have to be packed full of everything I could possibly crave – including those delicious brownies we still had tucked away in the fridge.

Now, just don't forget the bag!

Before even pulling into the parking lot at the café, I was daydreaming about lunch. My mouth watered, and my tummy rumbled. I was starving. That was pretty much the way I felt with Laurie too. Always hungry.

At least that was something I had expected rather than all this pregnancy brain and unbearable cravings. I spotted what looked like my mom's van in the parking lot and parked next to it. I gazed out the passenger side window and saw the pink fuzzy dice hanging from her rearview mirror.

I smiled, thinking it was just a fun coincidence that my mom had chosen this place for lunch today as well.

I unhooked the baby carrier from the car seat and plopped it onto the stroller base, loving that convenience too, and pushed her toward the quaint little French café. I swear, I could smell that baked chicken and mushroom already. Someone else had ordered it, and my craving heightened. "Yummy…" I said, and Laurie giggled.

Then I spotted my mom and Paula both sitting out on the patio together. I grinned.

What are those two up to?

"Hey!" I called to them, changing the direction I was pushing Laurie to meet them outside. Paula's two kids were squirming next to her. The baby propped in a car seat and Danny mesmerized by my mom's jangling bracelets. Paula was dressed in a pretty silk blouse with a spring floral print on it. She was flushed from the exertion of corralling the kids.

There was an empty chair waiting for me with space for the stroller next to it. I plopped down, ready for that chicken. "Well, this is a pleasant surprise, Mom. I didn't know you were joining us."

"Well, we both have something exciting to tell you," my mom said, practically shaking. She was dressed like a gypsy today. Not sure why, but my mom always did something kind of random with her wardrobe. She's quite a character.

"Oh, both of you?" I asked, trying to figure out what sort of secret Paula and my mother could possibly be sharing.

The waitress deposited a basket of breadsticks on the table, she took my drink order, and I immediately ordered lunch too. I couldn't wait for that chicken and mushroom dish.

Paula handed Danny a bread stick, and Laurie pounded her fists on the table, demanding attention.

"Yes, darling," my mom said sweetly. "You too." She handed Laurie a soft breadstick, and drool ran down her chin.

Is my insatiable hunger rubbing off on her, I wondered, as I wiped my own chin, hoping to find it dry.

Thankfully, I had not yet been reduced to a drooling fool, but I feared if my food didn't arrive soon, I was in trouble.

I turned to Paula and my mom. "Okay, ladies, so what's the big news?" I asked. "You got me feeling anxious!"

"You know Vicente's play?" my mom asked, and I nodded.

How could I forget?

Vicente Domingo was another PI in San Francisco who'd snagged one of my most prized clients—a high profile criminal defense attorney—because they were first cousins.

Vicente was also a playwright, and after helping me out on a case a couple of months ago, practically forced me to agree to a staged reading of his play. But somehow I wiggled out of it, claiming, of course, that I was too busy as a PI and full time mom to fuss with the theater.

My mom had eagerly stepped in, and from what I gathered, Vicente was quite smitten with my mom's performance.

"Yeah, how's it going?" I asked.

"Great!" she exclaimed. "But, Paula's the one with the exciting news on that front."

"Oh?" I asked, looking at Paula.

"Your mom got me hired for designing the set!" Paula shrieked, and I squealed excitedly for her. Paula was an interior designer by trade, but she'd had to sit out of the business for a bit during her pregnancies and while living abroad due to her husband's job. Recently, she'd been slowly rebuilding her clientele.

She was doing well for a startup, but it was still just a startup – so any job booking was something to celebrate.

"You guys, that's awesome!" I said. "Congratulations, Paula!"

"The set looks amazing," Mom said, winking. "Although, it's still a work in progress, but I can see Paula's vision coming to life, and it's astounding."

"They are putting the final touches on the set as we speak," Paula said. "When I left for lunch, they told me it should be just about done by the time we get back. I was hoping you and your mom wanted to get a sneak peek of my work after lunch today?"

"Absolutely!" I said. "I am so happy for you, Paula!"

"A lot of people are going to see this play," Paula said. "The tickets are already sold out, but don't worry, I got you and Jim some tickets so that you can come see your mom perform."

"Already sold out?" I questioned. "We are talking about a play written by Vicente, right?"

"Well, the concept sounds very exciting and intriguing," my mom said. "But the play itself is... well... silly. It's not supposed to be, but some of the one-liners are really corny. It's supposed to be a drama, but it comes off a little cheesy at times. Even melodramatic."

"What's the play about?" I asked just as the server arrived with my drink.

Food. I wanted food.

Patience, Kate. Patience.

"A small-town PI who is supposed to be working on a cheating husband case. Takes place in the Sierra Foothills. He winds up falling for the client, and the two of them get together, and she mysteriously dies. Then, the PI has to leave town and hide out in the big city," her mom said.

"That does sound very dramatic. But the lines are cheesy?" I questioned.

My mom then did a little southern drawl. "Oh, Vinnie, I just wanna run away! I don't wanna be here no more! No more, Vinnie! Let's just you and me go away together. Paint the town red. Spend a lifetime out in the big city where none of these hillbilly folks can bother us no more! Besides, I'm tired of listenin' to all them crickets chirping away every night. I'd rather go to sleep to the sound of your breathing and the busy city outside my window!"

I nearly spit my water out. "Oh, please tell me that's not really one of your lines?"

"It is," Paula said, smirking. "I had the pleasure of listening to everyone run lines the other day while I was working on the set."

"That's hilarious," I said, giggling. "Poor Vicente... wait... Vinnie... is the character based on him?"

"I don't think so," my mom said.

"I wouldn't be surprised. I mean, he's a nice guy and everything, but he does love himself so," Paula said, chuckling.

17

"I know what you mean," I agreed.

Mom shrugged. "Well, maybe the *character* was inspired by himself a little, but he's told me the story is just a story. No truth to it."

Interesting. Very interesting. Vicente Domingo has always been a bit of a question mark to me. I'd been meaning to look into him a bit more.

Finally, our food arrived, and I couldn't concentrate on much else until I'd wolfed down the entire serving.

CHAPTER 3

*a*fter lunch, we caravanned over to the theater. On the drive, Laurie giggled and did her cutsie baby babble, putting me in an unusually chirpy mood.

We pulled into the back-parking lot of the theater, and I parked next to Paula and my mom who'd ridden there together.

I scurried out of the driver's seat and removed Laurie's portable car seat from the car. As soon as she got near me, she went straight for my earring.

"Ack!" I yelped, taking hold of her tiny wrist. "Sweetie, no – no!" I said, and my mom hurried over to step in to my aid.

"Yeah, I never wear earrings anymore," Paula said as she locked up her car.

"Laurie, let go of your mommy's earring!" my mom said, laughing a little too hard at my uncomfortable misfortune.

"I suppose I should know better by now," I groaned as my mom wiggled my earring and the lower half of my ear free of my daughter's tight grasp. I passed Laurie off to my mom so I could rub my tender earlobe, then remove my earrings altogether. I tossed them into my front seat cup holder, as Laurie squealed and giggled about what she'd just done.

"You little stinker," I said to Laurie.

Paula pointed to her teal necklace. "Check this out," she said. "Definitely going to snag you one of these for your next baby shower."

"What? A plastic necklace?" I asked.

"It's a teether," Paula said, taking Laurie from my mom. Laurie went straight for it, biting and drooling all over Paula. "They're super cute; I even wear them when I don't have my little ones with me. They're stylish necklaces made out of safe teething materials. So, you can still get a little dressed up without having to worry about little ones snapping the chain on your nice jewelry."

"Don't think that would work in an earring form," I said, still rubbing my sore earlobe. "I swear, she just tried to rip my whole ear off!"

"That's not even close to the worst thing she'll ever do to you," my mom said, laughing. "Glad mine's grown up now so that I can just be grandma." She patted my head and strutted toward the theater.

Paula snapped Laurie's portable car seat onto the stroller for me. From the back of the stroller I nabbed a box of baby wipes and handed one to Paula to rid her necklace of my child's slobber.

Paula laughed, and removed the necklace. She handed it down to Laurie who eagerly reached for it, her eyes wide. "Tell you what, you just take that one," Paula said. "I have plenty at home. Laurie seems to like it anyway."

Paula pulled her children out of her mini-van and securely fastened them into her double stroller. Both were sound asleep.

"How do you do that?" I asked.

She laughed. "I'm a baby whisperer, don't you know?"

"I guess," I said pushing Laurie toward the theater's back exit.

Paula giggled. "I also put the heater on super high in the car and play this new agey meditation tape on the stereo. They fall asleep in record time, but I have to be careful or it puts me to sleep too."

We chuckled together as we strolled our little ones through the back door of the theater. "So, let's see this super awesome set I've heard so much about," I said.

Paula grinned as we entered the back of the building near the actor's greenrooms, and I hear a number of voices – they seemed to be running lines. I peered into the greenroom, and sure enough there were a handful of actors running through lines while waiting for their director.

Upon seeing my mom, a few of them hopped up excitedly, requesting she run lines with them.

"Easy there, everyone," my mom said. "Give me five minutes. I'm about to give my daughter the grand tour."

"Oh, so this is your daughter?" a handsome older man asked, standing. "Peter Jones. I'm playing your mother's other half in the play." The slightly gray-haired gentleman approached me, and extended his hand to shake mine. He didn't quite make it to me though, before getting distracted by Laurie. "Oh, wow, she's adorable!"

I grinned. The best way to any mother's heart is to shower her children with compliments.

"Thanks," I said. "So you're playing Vicente's leading man?"

"In other words, I'm playing a weird version of Vicente," Peter said, winking slightly. "I'm still a little nervous about the direction the director chose to take. I don't like disappointing the playwright."

"I've been told the director has turned this thing into a comedy?" I question, and Peter nods – a few other actors snicker.

"It's not your fault, Peter," a woman with bright orange hair said, getting up to come greet us. "Director Ricky made the call."

"I write myself," Peter explained. "So, messing with someone's vision this much, well, it feels kind of unfair. I would hate to see something I wrote turn out so differently than what I envisioned."

The woman shrugged and then looked at Paula and me. "I'm Natalie. I bring the character Jezebel to life."

"Jezebel?" I questioned.

"Yeah, not the best name choice, but the character does run a dive bar," Nate said, laughing. "I am basically a bar maid in the play."

"So, the play takes place at a dive bar?" I asked.

"Most of it does," Paula said. "You ready to check out my set?"

"Oh, so this is the set designer!" a third actor jumped up. "I'm Tony Yipps. I'm the one who sent you the color swatches."

"That was you?" Paula said, smiling. "Thanks for the recommendations. I think they went perfectly with the background."

"Have you seen it yet?" Tony asked.

"Not yet, we're headed there now," Paula said.

"Let's all go," Peter suggested. "We can run through blocking before Ricky gets here."

We all scooted down the hall toward the stage wings, and when we stepped out onto stage, it was, well, incredible.

Stage left was the bar. It looked positively gorgeous. The play, from what I skimmed during lunch, takes place in northern California – Gold Country. The backdrop for the stage was a mountain range and some elegantly painted bright yellow trees. Stage right, a sort of makeshift garage look.

"Wow!" Paula shrieked excitedly. "They finished putting it together! Hold on, I have a few boxes in the car for some of the final detail pieces."

Paula scurried off, and I stood center stage staring at the beautiful design. I could hardly believe how beautiful it looked.

"I like the way she set up the garage," my mom said, pointing toward the rusty front half of a car that poked out onto the stage. "All the set crew has to do to move half the set on and off stage is put the car in neutral and roll it back – the rest of the garage part of the set is on wheels and drilled to the back of the car. It's so easy to move on and off stage despite how complicated the look is."

"Clever," I said and then looked at the bar. The bar side of the stage was set up on a wooden platform about a foot high. It could also be easily moved on and off stage with a simple pull or push despite its large structure. The color contrast between the bright backdrop and the darker bar and garage scene was simply stunning.

Paula arrived seconds later with a large box, and she added a few details. A stained-glass window for the back of the bar and some old beer and whiskey bottles filled with water and food coloring. She had brought a can of paint, and she carefully dabbed areas in the garage to make it appear more rustic and covered in oil.

When she stepped back, finished with her masterpiece, the entire crew started clapping excitedly.

"Paula, simply amazing," Tony said. "I'm glad they hired you."

"Very talented," Nate said. "I especially love my little bar." She stood up and hurried behind the bar. "This right here is my character's personal spot."

"I have arrived!" a man's voice called from the audience.

"Ricky!" my mother called. "Oh, Kate, this is Director Ricky. He is doing a fabulous job, if I do say so myself. Ricky, this is my daughter Kate, and my granddaughter Laurie."

Ricky was a fairly young guy. He was younger than some of his cast members, but he had a certain commanding tone about him that let me know he was in charge.

"A pleasure, Ms. Kate," he said and smiled down at Laurie. "Hey, cutie," he said and then looked up at Paula. "Paula, I have to say, I'm in love with this set."

"Thanks for the opportunity," Paula said.

"Of course," he said and reached into his coat pocket. "Here, these are for you. Tickets for the after party on opening night." He looked at me. "Would you like to come?"

"Me?" I questioned.

"Your mom is one of the stars of the show," he said and reached into his pocket, pulling out two tickets.

"You are already coming to opening night," Paula said. "Plus, a little birdy told me that *Cassandra's Cookies* is catering the party."

My eyes widened. "Cassandra's Cookies? As in—"

"As in the café that you've had Jim run out to, I don't know, eight times since you've become pregnant," my mom said, giving me a playful nudge.

A vision of the dark chocolate brownies with the purple icing began to dance in front of my eyes. I had some at home in the fridge, but I was down to just two now.

"Speaking of which," Director Ricky said. "I need one of you to run by the café to drop off our catering contract. It's in my office now, but we need to get right to work on our tech rehearsal."

"I could do that for you," I said. "I go right by there on my way home."

"Are you sure?" Ricky questioned, taking a glance at Laurie – probably not wanting it to be too much of a burden.

"It's no problem," I said. "Besides, I can restock my brownie supply while I'm there, since its' all baby number two is letting me eat." I patted my barely noticeable baby bump.

He smiled. "Well, I really appreciate that." He handed me the contract, and I stuffed it into the stroller.

Okay pregnancy brain, don't let me forget to do that, I told myself.

The front doors to the theater flung open, and we all glanced up to see Vicente stepping in from the lobby. He was striking in a black leather jacket and tight jeans. Under one arm, he carried his motor-cycle helmet, and with his free hand, he ruffled his thick dark wavy hair. He graced us with a smile that would make a school girl blush, and even Paula's cheeks got a bit rosy.

I smacked her arm, and she giggled, mouthing to me. "I can't help it, he's so hot."

The director rushed over to Vicente. "Ah, Mr. Domingo!" Ricky exclaimed. "Welcome to tech rehearsal."

Vicente glanced around and nodded to the cast and crew, making his way down the aisle toward the stage. When his eyes landed on me, he gave me his special cat-that-ate-the-canary smile. The one that told me he thought I'd made a dreadful mistake not to have taken him up on his offer as the lead.

A man like Vicente Domingo could never imagine giving up the limelight.

"Hello Kate," he said.

I wiggled my fingers at him. "Congratulations, I understand the show's already sold out."

He gave me a condescending nod, as if I should have expected nothing less.

He glanced up at the stage, smiling and looking quite satisfied. "Just thought I would come take a peek at the set, and I have to say, it's looking good."

"Glad you like it," Paula said.

"Very sophisticated – just what I was going for," he mused, and I could sense several of the actors cringe. They weren't kidding. Domingo still had no idea that Ricky had turned this drama into a comedy. Ricky did not seem at all fazed.

"You coming opening night, I hope?" Ricky asked, smiling like he was not secretly plotting to put on a joke performance of what seemed to be Domingo's pride and joy.

"Wouldn't miss it for the world," Domingo said. "I will be here front and center."

While the cast and crew got ready for their tech rehearsal, my stomach began to rumble.

How can I even be hungry again?

But it wasn't hunger exactly, it was the purple icing brownies calling my name.

So I bid my mom and Paula farewell, told them to break a leg, and headed out with Laurie in tow.

Confession? The café wasn't exactly on my way home. It was about five minutes out of the way, but honestly, I had to make sure I had plenty of those amazing brownie's in stock for my next stakeout. I couldn't miss another money shot.

Laurie giggled and played with her stylish teether on the way there, and I plopped her into her stroller again before we headed inside. The outside of the café was painted bright orange. It was very colorful and fun; I hadn't ever actually been here myself. Jim had been doing the supportive daddy thing – running out constantly to help me satisfy my intense cravings.

Once inside though, I was a bit taken aback by the wild color palate. The walls were a mix of fire-engine red, with yellow and orange swirls, so much so that it made my head spin.

I made my way over to the counter, eagerly scanning the display case for my preferred treat. Disappointment tugged at me when I didn't see any of those brownie's on display.

The woman behind the counter had red hair, pulled up tight in a bun. She smiled. "May I help you?"

"I'm looking for a certain brownie... It's dark chocolate with purple icing?" I questioned.

"Kate?" she asked, taking me by surprise.

"Um… yes?"

"I knew it," she said. "You're Jim's wife, right? He comes in here three times a week to get you those brownies. I'm Cassandra, the owner."

I smiled. "Oh! I'm so embarrassed," I said, laughing.

"Hold on, I have a batch for you in the back that just got taken out of the oven. I need to wait a few more minutes before I ice them," she said. "That okay?"

"That's fine, oh, and here. This is the contract for the local theater. I guess you are catering their cast party?" I reached down and grabbed the contract out of the bottom of the stroller, handing it over to her.

She smiled and thanked me, not really questioning why I would have it. I watched her step back into the kitchen, probably to file the contract, and I sat down by the window. A few minutes later, she reappeared with a small plate and a to-go box.

"Tell you what, it's on the house," Cassandra said, smiling as she put the small plate with a brownie in front of me. "The to-go one's too."

She's so nice!

"Wow, thank you!" I said, happily grabbing the fork she had placed by my plate.

"Oh, that must be Laurie!" she said, bending down to take a look inside the stroller. "So cute. She looks like her daddy."

I smile. "She really does. I'm guessing Jim has told you about Laurie?"

"Well, he's been here enough for us to have chatted a few times," Cassandra said, smirking slightly. "I don't get a lot of male customers coming in and ordering chocolate in bulk like that. I finally asked him what was up, and he told me about his pregnant wife's cravings. He showed me a picture of Laurie. Super cute girl you got there."

"Thanks," I said, grinning.

"So," she said, standing upright. "Are you in the play?"

"No, but my mom is. I'll be going to opening night, and the

director was kind enough to invite me to the after party, so I figured I could bring the contracts by for him – and get me another one of these amazing brownies too."

Cassandra laughed. "Well, tell you what, they weren't in the order, but I'll throw in some of those brownies at the party so you can look forward to having them after the show."

"Thanks," I said, smiling. "You are too sweet."

"I try to keep my customers happy," she said. "Especially ones who come in and order a dozen brownies every few days."

CHAPTER 4

*B*y the time evening came, I was feeling absolutely miserable. I'd been by the toilet for the remainder of the afternoon waiting for everything to just come up, but it wouldn't happen for me. Not only was I nauseous, but my head hurt and my whole body was aching. It was not the best pregnancy day. This pregnancy was giving me a run for my money.

Laurie was being a little angel for me, though. She sat and played in the living room all afternoon Whiskers and the new teething necklace that that cat seemed to like as much as Laurie did. Meanwhile, I tried not to curl up in a ball and cry. I could see Laurie from my station by the toilet in the hall bathroom, so it worked out somewhat decently since she was so content playing and rolling around on the floor.

I knew most women dealt with morning sickness, but for some reason, mine was coming in the late afternoon. When I finally, ahem, relieved my stomach and threw up everything, I was feeling a little better but not entirely. I literally crawled from our hall bath to the living room floor where Laurie was playing and rolled over onto my back, staring up at the ceiling.

I patted my stomach. "You're a little monster, you know that?" I told my tiny bump.

Then I heard the sound of keys jingling outside, and I was overcome with relief. The door opened, and there was my knight in shining armor.

Jim smiled down at me; I'm sure I looked like a hot mess. My shirt was disgustingly stained and smelly. My hair was let down and in a complete mess, and the little bit of eyeliner I had put on that morning had run down my cheeks during my uncontrollable dry-heaving and had dried and started to crack along my cheeks.

"Rough day?" Jim asked, a slight chuckle in his voice. He threw his stuff down by the door, not even bothering to find everything's proper location like he usually did. Then he crawled down onto the floor next to Laurie, Whiskers, and me and gave me a reassuring pat on the shoulder. Laurie cooed and held her arms up to him.

"Rough afternoon, mostly," I said. "I was fine this morning. Went to lunch with mom and Paula – got us tickets to the show mom's in. And, I got after party tickets too. Came home this afternoon and just suddenly started feeling like baby number two was trying to murder me by clawing his way out."

"That sounds… lovely," Jim said.

I smirked at him from where I was still lying flat on my back. He sat near my head, his legs crossed, with Laurie in his lap cooing away like the happy little girl she usually was.

"I wasn't like this with Laurie," I said. "I don't think I can take much more of this."

"You're tougher than you give yourself credit for," Jim said. "The nausea stuff is only the first trimester, right?"

I smacked him. "That's still a few more weeks," I groaned. "But, not everyone is that lucky. Morning sickness can last the entire pregnancy and this is pretty bad."

"Don't be so negative. Everything is going to fine," Jim said. He smiled down at me. "Tell you what. Why don't you go relax? I'll handle Laurie. I could use some daddy-daughter time, anyway. Go take a bath."

"I'm not supposed to take baths," I said.

"You're not supposed to take hot baths," he corrected. "Just don't take your normally hot-sauna type bath, okay? Just sit and soak in some lukewarm water, light a candle. Whatever you have to do to unwind."

"You are amazing, you know that?" I said, and he lent me a hand to help me sit upright. I was definitely going to take him up on his offer. I needed to wind down bad after the sort of afternoon I'd had. I stood up and then bent down to give him a quick kiss before retreating back to our bedroom.

I loved our bathroom at the house; the house was a typical home in the parkside district of San Francisco. Built in the 1920s, the previous owners had kept the beautiful claw foot tub. When we'd first moved in, Jim and I had the tub refinished, and now it just sparkled and shined like the gem it really was.

One of the things I loved about it, was that it was taller than most modern-day tubs, so I sit comfortably and feel as if I'm reclined, and let's face it, what woman doesn't enjoy a good soak?

I let the water run for a little bit. This to me was one of the biggest downsides of being pregnant. I love sitting in steaming hot water with bubbles and taking a small glass of wine with me – it was a great way to wind down after long, stressful days.

But, being pregnant, you have certain restraints. Hot water could be bad for the baby if it raises your body temperature, so the water had to be lukewarm at best. Bubble baths give me an increased risk of infection which could also hurt the baby, so I would just have to sit in plain water.

And, of course, wine was not recommended except in small doses, but I just avoided alcohol completely while pregnant. So, my hot bubble bath with a glass of wine was really going to be just me sipping a Yoo-hoo from a straw while sitting in lukewarm water, but, hey, I would take what I could get.

As the tub filled up with water, I started to get undressed. And, well, that's when I had the single biggest scare of my entire life. I pulled down my drawers, and there was blood. More than just a little bit – not enough to go into full panic, but enough to make my heart jump up into my throat.

"Jim!" I'm pretty sure I screamed louder than I should have. I heard him come stomping through the house, Laurie in tow, like he thought I had fallen and hit my head or something.

By the time he got to the bathroom, I had thrown on a robe and had investigated the source of the blood glop. I was definitely bleeding – fairly heavily, might I add. I didn't even have to say anything because my pants and underwear were sitting on the floor in front of the tub.

Jim instantly went pale, and he put Laurie down. "I'm taking you to the hospital," he said. "I'm going to call Kenny, get dressed."

He switched into autopilot, I think. It was his way of keeping himself from panicking. Kenny darted over before I could even get my purse together. By the time I came out of the back bedroom, Kenny was already wearing the teething necklace and playing with Laurie on the floor. He looked up at me with this concerned gaze while Jim threw on a jacket and snagged the car keys.

"Are you all right, Kate?" Kenny asked.

"I think so… I don't know…" I said, quickly spitting out a thank you for rushing over so quickly while Jim ushered me out the door and helped me into the car.

We didn't speak to each other much on the way to the hospital. Jim reached for my hand at every red light, and it seemed we hit all of them.

I'd virtually zero problems with my first pregnancy. Why was this happening?

Maybe all of my dry heaving from earlier hurt the baby, I thought – ready to instantly blame myself.

The thought that I might be having a miscarriage made me want to curl up and cry. My hands were shaky, and when I glanced over at Jim, I could tell he was worried. His eyes were glossy, and his stare was very intense as he looked out at the road in front of us.

"Should I call Dr. Green?" I asked.

He nodded, and I pulled out my cell phone. I had her on speed dial, but her office was closed for the evening. I left her a message with her answering service then shrugged at Jim.

A few minutes later, I received a text from Dr. Green's office telling me to go straight to the hospital and that she would meet us there in the emergency wing.

I was really relieved to see Dr. Green pulling up at the same time as us. She smiled and greeted us and immediately starting asking me questions. She did, however, sound reassuring as we walked into the ER, and for that I was grateful.

She led us out of the waiting room and down a series of connecting halls toward her practice's office area. In an instant, Jim and I were in a room.

The first thing she did was hand me an awful hospital gown. While I changed, she scrubbed her hands, then rubbed some goop on my belly to check for the baby's heartbeat.

Anxiety seemed to be choking me, and I bit back tears as I looked at Jim.

I was so grateful he'd been at home when this happened. He stood by me, holding my hand, while we waited patiently for Dr. Green. Then, we heard the sound that made both Jim and me exhale in relief.

Our baby's heartbeat.

"Sounds like your baby is just fine, but I'm going to do a blood test and do a cervical check to make sure everything's okay," Dr. Green said, but then she paused for a second. She continued listening to the heartbeat, moving the little device across my stomach. "Hold on a second, there, Kate... I think I'm picking up a second heartbeat..."

"Wait, what?" Jim asked, suddenly becoming very lively. "You mean you're picking up Kate's heartbeat?"

"No, I mean there might be a second baby in there," Dr. Green said. She put the little device aside and reached over to the ultrasound machine; it rolled toward the chair where I was seated, and I leaned back. "You're due for your second ultrasound next week anyway. Let's take a look."

My heart raced. Twins?

She turned the light off in the room. There was a monitor display in the corner for Jim and me to look at. Sure enough, I spotted a little baby that still looked a little more peanut-like than baby wiggling around.

"Oh, yeah, there's two in there," Dr. Green said.

"What! Where?" Jim demanded. I couldn't tell if he was horrified or excited.

She pointed toward the screen. "That second baby is hiding behind the first one, but you can see three arms on the... hold on, they're moving. Yup, there you go."

I could see two heads. They were squished together, their arms were so tiny compared to the rest of them right now, but I could see both of their shapes clearly.

Dr. Green clicked a button on the ultrasound to capture the clear shot. "Congratulations," she said. "You're having twins. I can't believe we didn't pick up that second heartbeat at your last visit."

I heard a dry-heaving sound erupt from Jim's throat, and his hand squeezed me tight. I looked over at him, and he was white as a ghost, but he was smiling... sort of.

"Jim? Are you okay?" I asked.

"Yeah, yeah," he said quickly, but he let go of me and sat down in the spare chair. "Twins," he said under his breath, and he started laughing uncontrollably.

Dr. Green looked from Jim to me. "It's a lot to take in, I know."

I didn't have time to deal with whatever Jim was going through at the moment. I was at least glad he was smiling, though. We hadn't planned on having a second baby so soon, but he had been really excited... but twins was a lot more than we had expected, so I was going to give him a minute to let it sink in before I go all pregnant angry Kate on him. I had something else on my mind.

"What about the blood?" I asked. "Are the babies okay?"

"They appear to be, but I'm going to check you over to be sure," she said and proceeded to turn the lights back on and get ready for an exam. Jim kept sitting in the chair looking like a deer in headlights. Before she could begin, a nurse knocked on the door and entered with the printed ultrasound.

Dr. Green handed it over to Jim so he could look at it while she conducted the exam. "Everything's looking good, Kate, but there is a lot of spotting down there," she said. "I'm going to have a nurse come in and draw some blood and then I'm going to have you wait downstairs in the ER for the lab results before I send you home, just to be safe. It sounds like it was a lot of blood, so I want us to be cautious, okay?"

"Thank you, Dr. Green," I said, and she left the room. While we were waiting for the nurse, I turned my head to look at Jim. "Jim?" I said, and he looked up at me with this goofy looking grin of his.

"Twins," he said.

"Yes, twins," I said and smiled. "Are you... okay with that?"

"Shocked, but yeah, baby," he said and stood up. "Sorry... I was just a little... surprised." He bent down and gave me a kiss, standing over me. He held the ultrasound picture out so we could both look. "There are definitely two little ones in there." He bent down and kissed my stomach. "You aren't hiding anymore in there, are you?" he asked, and I laughed nervously.

"Not funny," I said, smirking.

A nurse arrived and drew a blood sample, and after a few more minutes, a second nurse arrived to cart me to a hospital room in a wheelchair. Jim walked behind, and after a few minutes we were left alone in the hospital room, with me propped up in the bed. My mind was running in a million different directions.

"Oh, I have to call Mom!" I suddenly wailed, and Jim gave me this pleading look. "What? Do you want to tell her?"

"Kind of," he said. Jim's parents were deceased, and he didn't have much of a family life, in fact, he thought of my mom as his own.

I was the one always calling mom with news. I told her the first time I was pregnant. Told her when we found out we were having a girl. And, I got to tell Mom about being pregnant for a second time. Jim didn't really have anyone he was as close to as my mom to call and give exciting news like this.

"Go ahead," I said, and he smiled and snagged his phone.

When he told her the news about my being pregnant with twins, I could hear my mom shrieking through the phone into Jim's ear from across the room.

I laughed, glad she was so excited. But, we were still in the ER. This was a time to be serious. Once I knew the babies were fine, I would celebrate.

After about an hour of waiting around, Dr. Green arrived wearing a serious expression.

My heart plummeted.

"Okay, so your test came back, and you have a low oxygen level in your blood," she began, pulling up a chair beside my hospital bed. She proceeded to ask me a series of questions about my health, exercise routine, and diet. Everything checked out. "Tell me a little more about the carbon monoxide poisoning you experienced last month," she said, and my stomach dropped.

Could my babies be hurt?

Dr. Green hadn't been the one to treat me for that incident. It'd been a doctor here at the ER. So, I gave her the rundown.

A psychopath had locked my mom in a steam room at a sauna and had filled it with carbon monoxide. I had gotten my mom out, but I had wound up collapsing after inhaling too much of the poison.

"Did you pass out? Were you unconscious?" Dr. Green asked. She flipped through my file, looking at the other physician's notes.

"Yes," I said. "But, the doctor said I was probably fine."

"I agree. The babies are likely fine," Dr. Green said. "A mild carbon monoxide poisoning will not normally cause harm to the fetus, but since you passed out, there is a chance it did affect them in some way. Right now, other than low oxygen in your bloodstream, there doesn't appear to be anything to worry about. But, we are going to have to keep a very close eye on you during this pregnancy, Kate. You and the babies, to make sure there have not been any serious, long-term effects."

I felt sick and angry and a million other emotions, but Dr. Green was very reassuring. Everything had looked fine on the ultrasound and during her inspection. And, other than a slightly low supply of oxygen in my blood, nothing came back unusual in the blood sample either when they tested it. So long as we were careful, the babies should be fine.

And, then she delivered the bad news: she wanted me to stay overnight at the ER and put me on oxygen until morning.

Great.

Jim insisted on staying with me, so he called Kenny who was more than willing to stay with Laurie – he was just glad to hear that I was okay, and he was almost as excited as Mom about my having twins.

TWINS?

We're having twins!

CHAPTER 5

a little over a week went by after my unfortunate visit to the ER before opening night of Domingo's play.

By that time, I was chomping at the bit to get out of the house. Jim had treated me like a hothouse flower and practically restricted me to bed rest.

I did get his permission to do one stakeout as long as I had someone with me. Kenny, it seemed, was now babysitting me instead of Laurie.

Kenny eagerly agreed to go on the stakeout and even packed us plenty of carbs and sugar. We had chips, coke, candy bars and enough Swedish Fish to survive a zombie apocalypse.

This time around, getting a snap of our lumberjack adulterer was easy peasy. They'd left the curtains open, and the shots I took were so compromising, I had to tell Kenny to look away.

The woman was young, wearing a slinky black negligee and blonde hair twisted into dreadlocks.

I'd returned home victorious, but exhausted, at 4 am and eagerly agreed to print the photos after the play. Now I stood checking my reflection in the mirror and couldn't deny the dark circles under my eyes from last night's stakeout.

"You look gorgeous," Jim said.

"Liar."

He chuckled. "Why do you say that? You're always beautiful to me."

The doorbell rang and Kenny strutted into the house, looking no worse for wear after pulling an all-nighter with me.

Ah to be seventeen again!

"Laurie's already asleep, Kenny, hopefully it'll be an easy night for you," Jim said.

Kenny sniffed around the room and looked disappointed.

I laughed. "Jim didn't grill anything tonight. There's an opening night reception at the play. So order pizza if you're hungry."

"Coolio," he said.

Kenny was always hungry, and being that his parents were vegan, didn't often get the chance to order pizza.

I grabbed Jim's arm as we made our way to the car. "You look super handsome, hot stuff," I said. I was so excited to be out on a date with my sexy husband that butterflies danced in my stomach. "We need more date nights."

He leaned and kissed me before opening my car door, "I know. I miss you. You know? I love our family, but sometimes I miss the just you and me part of it."

I cradled his face. "It's always you and me, honey."

He smiled and inhaled the scent of my hair. "You and me against the world. That's right. I love you, Kate."

<><><>

JIM and I met Galigani at the theater. Thanks to Paula we had great seats. Unfortunately, she was missing opening night and the after party; her kids and husband had all come down with the flu. I felt for her – especially since she had designed the set, but she had managed to snag two tickets for closing night, which meant I would be back to see the play again with her at a later date. Knowing that I was going to be sitting through this thing twice made me really hope it was good and entertaining.

The lights in the theater dimmed, and the curtains opened. I couldn't resist texting Paula just to tell her how amazing the set looked before politely turning off my cell phone as the instructions over the speakers had requested before the show had started.

On stage were Peter and Nate. Peter's character was dressed in a leather jacket as he sat down at the bar; he was playing the fictionalized version of Vicente Domingo, and I was excited to get a snap shot of Domingo's life even if it was supposedly fictionalized.

Vinnie ordered a cup of coffee, and Nate played it off like an annoyed bar tender. Next, Tony entered – he was playing the role of the cheating husband. The scene unfolded as Tony flirted with the steamy redheaded actress in front of Vinnie. While the two flirted, the all silent character Vinnie snapped photos.

It was supposed to be a serious scene – the undercover PI taking photos of his man, but the actors played it off almost like a photo-shoot – a little gag at the end in which the pair intentionally posed made the audience snicker.

Jim nudged me, and I looked to where he was nodding. A few rows in front of us was Domingo, and he looked positively irate. The first scene, and already Domingo was fuming. I thought of one of the scenes later in the play I had witnessed my mom run lines for the other day, and I cringed.

As much Vicente and I locked horns, I still felt a little bad for him. His vision was being picked apart on stage and turned into a lame comedy act. I didn't blame my mom or the actors – it had been the director's decision.

The next scene was even worse. Back at the bar was the cheat, the adulteress, and Nate still playing the bartender. When the adulteress headed to the ladies room, Nate's character leaned over the bar.

"Hey, Howie, that fella who was in here earlier... I think he snapped some photos of you and the side chick," she mused, and several of the ensemble characters – biker bar types – all glanced up from the various tables set up on stage.

"What!" Tony yelped at the top of his lungs and jumped up.

I heard music. "Oh no," I said under my breath. Not a musical number. An unscripted musical number!

Having had run lines with my mom more than once for this thing, I know Domingo's original script didn't include any musical numbers. Everyone was clapping and dancing, Tony was signing a ridiculous song that keyed the audience in on the fact that his character and his wife had a prenuptial agreement, that he thought he was being black-mailed, and that he was a big-shot powerful man in town. The whole thing, to make matters worse, was to the tune of the song *Gaston* from Disney's *Beauty and the Beast.*

Jim leaned over in the middle of a chorus and whispered, "Is there supposed to be music in Domingo's play?"

"No," I said, shaking my head. The audience was laughing and clapping along to what was basically a rewrite of the tavern scene from the Disney classic. I glanced over, and I could see that Domingo had completely sunk down in his seat in utter humiliation.

A few other hilarious scenes, followed by the big finale.

The audience clapped and gave the actors a standing ovation. After the play ended and the audience members cleared out, the lobby was opened up for the after party. Vicente was there, speaking harshly in a corner with the director.

I decided not to linger. Vicente was probably ready to strangle him for the betrayal. Instead, Jim, Galigani, and I mingled with Mom and some of her fellow cast members.

"That was... awful..." Peter said under his breath to Mom, Jim, and me. "I felt horrible. The writer was devastated. I could see him sinking down in his chair the whole time."

"The audience loved it," my mom said to reassure him.

Nate shook her head. "It was pretty bad. I've been telling Ricky since day one that this was a terrible idea. The musical number especially."

"I love the musical number," Jim said, and I stepped on his foot discreetly. He smirked and gave me a sideways glance.

"Yeah, you sure can dance, Nate," Tony said, smirking.

"The audience would have liked it just as much as a drama," Nate said. "It wasn't written to be a comedy. I feel like we just slapped the writer in the face."

"Let me show you the backstage," Mom said to Galigani, putting an arm through his.

They left our little group, and Jim whispered in my ear, "Aw, they're so cute together."

"Jim!" a familiar voice called, and Jim and I spun around to see a woman with fiery red hair and a baker's apron staring back at us.

It was Cassandra from Cassandra's Cookies. I smiled at her; she and her workers had just finished setting up the dessert table, and I guess she had stopped by to say hello.

"Cassandra," Jim said in this low, annoyed tone that caused me to feel a bit uncomfortable. It was so... rude... and so unlike Jim.

Cassandra ignored him and just smiled in my direction. "Hey, Kate, good to see you again. How were those brownies?"

"Amazing," I said. "As always."

"Wait... when did you two meet?" Jim asked.

"I went by the shop last week to deliver the catering contract for the director," I said.

Jim's face flushed, and he crossed his arms. "I didn't know you were catering," he said angrily.

Why is he angry?

Something was wrong. A sixth sense buzzed in my head. Why was he being rude to Cassandra?

I had been sending him to her café a lot to get those brownies. Had they had some sort of spat?

Cassandra, polite as ever, ignored Jim and continued to smile at me. "Well... anyway... I'm glad you liked the brownies. I was sure to put out a plate of them. I heard you were having twins?"

"How did you hear that?" Jim spat and I couldn't help but elbow him. My goodness, that tone of his!

"Paula told me," Cassandra said, putting her hands on her hips. "Do we have a problem, Jim?" she asked.

"No," he said.

"Okay, then," she said, shaking it off. "Well, anyway, yeah. Paula told me – she came by to taste test the raspberry and cream cheese blintzes for the party." Cassandra motioned to the table filled with delectable treats

I laughed. "Yum, I'll have to try those next," I said.

Cassandra smiled at me and then gave Jim a queer look. With that she headed off to chat to some others who were circling the dessert table.

"What was that about?" I snapped at Jim.

"It's nothing," he said in a tone that told me he definitely didn't want to talk about it, so I dropped it for the time being.

We were there to enjoy a party, so I wasn't going to let petty stuff spoil the evening. Jim was normally a friendly and personable guy. I figured something must be up to make him act that way.

I squeezed his arm, letting him know I was giving him the benefit of the doubt.

The party continued, and apart from Vicente sulking in a corner, it was a lot of fun. We mingled, ate some amazing food, and of course once I had properly dined I headed for that dessert table.

I took one bite of that brownie with the purple icing and had to spit it out quickly into my napkin. Nope!

Craving done!

In fact, I was a bit repulsed by it. I suppose I'd had one too many. I tossed my napkin in the trash, glancing around hoping no one had noticed.

Suddenly, I heard people shouting over in the corner. "Call 911!" someone wailed.

"She's not breathing!" called another.

I hurried over, and there she was. A woman wearing a *Cassandra's Cookies* apron sprawled out on the floor.

"Is she unconscious?" someone asked.

"Is there a doctor in the house?" another called out.

Vicente rushed over. "Back up. Give her some air," he demanded. "Let me help. I know CPR."

The crowd parted for him, and he dropped to his knees next to her. I got a good look at the woman, her blonde dreadlocks splayed across the hardwood floor.

My stomach churned.

I was certain she was dead.

And, to make matters worse, I knew her.

CHAPTER 6

$\mathcal{A}$n ambulance arrived and took over the CPR from Vicente. They spoke in hushed tones to each other about the woman's pulse or lack thereof.

The paramedics loaded her onto a stretcher and hauled the woman out of the theater post haste.

The crowd buzzed around in shock, the decibel level of their distress growing to an ear-shattering crescendo.

"A heart attack?" Someone asked.

"But she's so young," another said.

"Could have been an aneurysm," a woman in pink tulle offered.

"Did she just die?" a man swirling a champagne flute asked.

Cassandra and the other employees at *Cassandra's Cookies*, which consisted of four others apart from Cassandra and the woman who'd collapsed, were all standing nearby wide-eyed with horror-stricken looks painted on their faces.

"What... what happened!" Cassandra at last exclaimed. "Morgan was fine five minutes ago!"

No one could be sure yet – but I suspected foul play.

Why? Because Morgan was the adulteress.

That's right. The man I'd been following around? Yeah, his mistress was the woman who'd just been taken to the hospital.

I looked around for Galigani, but he and mom were nowhere to be found so I sent him a quick text to get to the lobby ASAP. I looked around with a keen sense about me. Our client wasn't here, and neither was creepy Raymond – our client's husband, the adulterer.

I had just taken pictures of Raymond and Morgan last night. Something wasn't right.

And, what are the chances of that anyway?

Jim rubbed my shoulder. "Aw, man," he said, shaking his head. "She's so sweet. I hope she'll be okay."

"Jim," I whispered, pushing him back so we weren't too close to anyone who might overhear. "Remember that client I was telling you about?"

"Sarah something or another?" Jim asked. "You and Kenny snapped a picture of her husband last night, right?"

"Right," I said and then nodded my head back toward Morgan. "Guess who the mistress was."

"Nooo!" he moaned in frustration for me. "Kate, do you think your client could be behind this?"

Before I could answer, Vicente Domingo crossed the room toward Cassandra.

"Ma'am," he said, putting his hand out toward Cassandra. "My name is Vicente Domingo, and I'm a private investigator. If you would like for me to look into—"

"Actually," Cassandra said, turning toward Jim and me. She hadn't raised her hand to shake, so she just left Vicente standing there awkwardly with his extended hand as she turned her back to him. "I was going to ask you, Kate. You're a PI, right?"

I grinned, flashing a smile in Vicente's direction. He frowned, then shook his head as if this was the most ridiculous thing he'd ever heard. He was about to speak, when I stepped in front of him and said, "And, I would love—"

"She'll think about it," Jim interrupted, and he touched my arm like he was trying to cart me away.

Vicente laughed and puffed up like a peacock. "Ah, no need to worry. If Kate is too busy with her babies, then—"

Now, I was mad.

Between Jim and Vicente, it would be a wonder if I'd ever land another client.

"No, Jim," I said. "I don't need to think about it." Then I turned to Vicente and hissed, "And I'm not too busy. I would love to help Cassandra out." I turned to her. "I'll do whatever I can to try to find out what happened to your employee."

Vicente huffed off, and a sour expression crossed Jim's face.

"Thank goodness," Cassandra said. "Thank you, Kate." She shook my hand, and I felt her trembling.

"Are you alright?" I asked.

Her grip tightened around my hand for a moment, and then she went limp; diving right into me and almost toppling me.

Jim caught me, but Cassandra crumpled to the floor.

"Oh my goodness," my mother shrieked, racing toward us.

Now the party went into full-blown panic mode. Whatever rumors had been circulating about Morgan quickly turned into *'someone was out to get everyone at this party.'*

I immediately thought about Vicente. Could he have been so angry about the production that he would do something to hurt these people?

But then why the caterers?

Had this been an accident? Or a coincidence?

Vicente rushed from across the room and administered CPR, while I dialed 911.

Clearly, whatever had just happened to Morgan was repeating itself with Cassandra. So Morgan had not collapsed from natural causes.

What then?

Was the food poisoned? The after party had begun right after the play – what were the odds someone could poison the food while we all milled around? I noticed the glasses around the room, almost everyone had a champagne flute or martini glass in hand. Could our perp have slipped Morgan and Cassandra a mickie?

If so, why?

As I was contemplating my next move, Galigani and mom burst into the theater.

"What's happened?" Mom demanded. "We saw an ambulance."

"Where have you been?" I asked.

I noticed the buttons on Mom's shirt were askew, and they both reddened. I regretted asking the question.

Goodness, they're worse than a couple of teenagers!

I quickly brought them up to speed, just as the theater doors flew open, and a few uniformed policemen stormed in. One of the officers took over the CPR duties until a crew of paramedics rushed in to attend to Cassandra.

Vicente came over to us, and I realized I had lost track of Jim.

Where was he?

He'd been quite a character all night. *Rude* was the word I kept thinking.

Now, the police seemed to be everywhere, swarming through the crowd, taking names and contact information.

"The first woman was dead," Vicente said. "I'm sure of it. I couldn't get any pulse. This one, I think will be okay."

Galigani nodded at him. "Yeah, I just heard the code over that officer's scanner." Galigani whispered, pointing to an officer near us, with a chirping walky-talky on his shoulder holster. "The first lady was DOA."

I bit my lip; I wanted to fill Galigani in on the first woman being our adulteress, but I didn't want to say anything in front of Domingo.

Instead, I glanced around the room for Jim and realized he wasn't in the lobby at all. A few people had trickled outside, so I wandered out into the parking lot where I spotted Jim speaking with an officer by a patrol car.

Nothing unusual – a lot of people were speaking with officers about what they had witnessed. I walked toward him, and the next thing I knew Jim was being put into the back of a patrol car.

What!

I bolted over. "Hey!" I shouted, approaching the officer. "What's going on? Why are you arresting my husband?"

"He's not under arrest, ma'am," the officer assured me. "We're just taking him to the station for additional questioning, and he's cooperating."

"Um... okay, but why?" I demanded.

Jim tapped on the glass of the back window. The officer opened up the back door so that I could speak with him.

"Jim! What's going on?" I asked, my voice shrill.

"Don't worry about it," he said. "Just go home, babe, and I'll be home later tonight."

"Um, I think I should worry about it, seeing as how Cassandra asked me to investigate this case," I said.

"Just go home," he said firmly. "I already sent a text to Galigani. Have him take you home."

The officer closed the door, politely tipped his hat to me, and got into the driver's seat. I stood there with my mouth wide open trying to figure out why in the world Jim would need to be taken in for additional questioning.

"Kate!" I heard my mom's voice, and I turned around to see her sprinting across the parking lot. Galigani chased after her.

"Kate, why are they taking Jim? Is he being arrested?" My mom looked near ready to keel over in shock.

"No, Mom," I said. "They just asked him to come in for some additional questioning, that's all."

"But, why?" Mom asked, her voice full of panic.

Galigani put a soothing hand on her shoulder. "He just has some information he wants to share with them, that's all."

"What information?" I demanded.

Galigani shrugged. "I don't know. That's all his text said. "I'm supposed to get you home."

"No way!" Mom said. "You drive Kate straight to that station. I'll follow."

"I can drive my own car, people!" I said, frustrated. "I'm pregnant, not blind!"

Mom waved a hand at me. "You're nervous, darling. It's not good to drive when you're nervous."

I decided it would be faster not to argue with them, so I agreed. Mom walked off to her car and I turned to Galigani.

"Before Cassandra passed out, she wanted me to investigate Morgan's death. Now, I feel torn between leaving the scene of the crime and following Jim to the station," I confessed. "Should one of us stay here and talk to the staff of *Cassandra's Cookies*?"

Galigani shook his head. "Family first. Morgan's already dead. Remember the living always come before the deceased." And with that, he put his hand on my back and ushered me toward my car.

On the short drive to the station, I filled Galigani in on Morgan.

"She's the woman in the photos?" he asked incredulously.

I nodded.

"We have to talk to Sarah ASAP," he said. "Do you have the photographs?'

"Yes, at the house. I can get the prints to you tonight."

"When we're done here, bring them to my office. I'll set up a meeting with Sarah for the morning," he said, pulling into the police station parking lot.

We parked next to Mom's car, and the three us of walked into the station together.

Once inside, Galigani told mom and me to sit down and he would find out what was happening with Jim. He knew half of the officers in this particular precinct from his days of serving on the force. And because of his upbeat personality, everyone loved him.

I tapped my foot impatiently, watching Galigani from across the station. My hormones were so out of whack, I felt like crying. Mom put her hand on my knee so that I would stop.

"I'm sure it's nothing, Kate," my mom said reassuringly. "It's Jim. What sort of trouble could Jim possibly have gotten himself into?"

She had an excellent point. I'd be surprised if someone told me my husband stomped on a butterfly. He was a softie, a total gentleman. He never made any enemies – not really. To think he could have done anything to get himself into trouble was ridiculous. After what felt like hours but was probably less than ten minutes, Galigani came over and sat down next to my mom and me on the bench.

"Well?" I asked.

"They're still questioning Jim," Galigani said. "But, they're almost through. He'll be able to leave in just a few minutes."

"But, why are they questioning Jim?" I asked.

"The woman who was poisoned, the one who is still alive and is at the hospital—"

"Cassandra?" I asked.

Galigani nodded. "Apparently, she and Jim had an altercation a few weeks ago," Galigani said. "The police were called to the scene."

"Wait, what?" I asked, sitting up straight. "Someone called the police on Jim!"

"Sounds like it," Galigani said.

"Why... why hasn't Jim told me!" I practically shouted, and Mom hushed me. I was drawing attention to myself. I took a deep breath.

My heart raced. "Do you know what happened?" I asked.

"They didn't give me details, but there was some sort of incident at the bakery. The two of them got into some verbal altercation, and Cassandra called the police to escort Jim off the property. She didn't press charges or anything, but it's on record," Galigani said. "And, since Cassandra was one of the victims, they wanted to talk to him about the incident."

"I can't believe Jim had to be escorted off a property," mom said. "That doesn't sound like Jim at all."

"We don't even know Cassandra!" I said. "What could they possibly have been arguing about?"

"It wasn't brownies, was it?" my mom asked, and I rolled my eyes.

"Come on! Jim didn't get into an argument over brownies," I said.

I know my cravings had been pretty bad with this pregnancy, but surely that would not lead Jim to getting into a fight with a bakery owner.

Something else was up, and I didn't like it.

My mom crossed her arms. "I just don't see Jim getting into an argument with someone he barely knows. Does he know Cassandra?"

"Not that I know of," I said, shaking my head. "He has been in and out of that bakery a lot in the past month or two picking up those stupid brownies for me. Maybe he got irritated one day when they didn't have them and had to wait around for a long time?"

"That still doesn't sound like Jim," Galigani said. "He's a patient man. He wouldn't just get mad and start yelling at someone over some brownies."

No, it didn't sound like Jim at all.

And, not telling me that there had been some sort of incident involving the police also didn't sound like Jim.

He and I never kept secrets from each other. Surely, I was missing something. Had he tried to tell me and I just shrugged it off or wasn't listening?

I had been really moody lately. I'd even gotten snippy with Vicente at the reception, and I normally tried to be polite despite his occasionally sexist attitude.

We sat around in silence until Jim finally came out.

Relief flooded me, and I hurried up to him. He scowled when he saw me.

"Kate, I thought I told you to go home? Everything's fine, okay? They just wanted to talk to me." He sounded really annoyed.

"Jim!" my mother shrieked. "Boy, you have some explaining to do!"

Jim frowned. "It's been a long night, Mom," he said gently. "I'd really just like to go home and go to bed, if that's okay?"

Sure, be polite to Mom and rude to me.

What did I do to make Jim angry with me?

CHAPTER 7

As soon as we were alone in the car, things between Jim and I got... well... weird. Never in our marriage had Jim ever been so distant. He refused to talk to me about the incident with Cassandra. He outright refused. I couldn't believe it. He never kept secrets from me.

"I just don't understand," I said, sulking in the passenger seat of our car. "You don't usually get into arguments with people. Especially not a total stranger. Why don't you want to talk about this if it was nothing?"

Jim gripped the steering wheel tight. I could tell that he was getting frustrated with me, but honestly, I was just so appalled by the idea of his being escorted off someone's property by police that I didn't care. Jim wasn't a rule breaker. He wasn't an aggressive personality type. And, the fact that this had happened several weeks before, and he had never told me, made me all the more upset.

He glanced my way. "Kate, drop it," he said, coldly.

"No," I spouted back.

"I told you, it wasn't a big deal, okay?" he said, raising his voice ever so slightly. Jim never raised his voice. "I went to get you some of those brownies you wanted, and Cassandra and I just got into an argument. The argument escalated into shouting, and Cassandra overreacted and called the police. The only reason I even stayed at the shop at that point was because I wanted to speak to the police and make sure they got everything down right. They walked me out of the shop. Obviously, it wasn't even that big of a deal because I wound up going back inside with the police, and she sold me the brownies, and we moved on. I've been back there twice since then to get you those stupid brownies, and we haven't had a problem. So, drop it, okay?"

He still didn't tell me what the argument was about. That was what bothered me. "You're not helping me with my investigation any," I said.

"I have nothing to do with your investigation," he snapped. "Unless you think I killed someone."

I sat upright. "Are you serious, Jim?" I questioned. I exhaled, loudly. "You know what, let's just forget about this for now. I'm done arguing with you."

"I told you not to take this case," he griped, and I chose not to respond because my response would have been loud and angry – it wasn't up to Jim which cases I took. He was just being uptight, and he didn't care to share with me why. If he would have given me an explanation as to why he didn't want me to take the case, I probably would have listened. But, he was being weird and secretive. I didn't care for it.

We were quiet for a while – which was uncomfortable. I had questions I wanted to ask him. Even though I obviously didn't think Jim was behind it, I still had to do my job. See if he knew anything, but he wasn't having it. I just sat there stewing in my seat, trying not to let my anger escalate.

After a while, he reached over and touched my hand – his silent way of apologizing without actually having to say it.

I sighed. "So, we haven't started thinking up names yet," I said, patting my stomach with my free hand.

I saw a smile creep across his face. "We don't even know if we're having boys or girls or one of each yet."

"Like we waited to find out what Laurie was before we started throwing names around," I said with a smirk. "What are you hoping for?"

"Honestly…" he said, glancing at me for a moment. "I just hope one of them is a boy."

I grinned. "Me too. Although, you would be an adorable daddy of a house full of girls."

"I really want a son," he said. "But, I'll be happy so long as they're healthy."

"I hope one of them is a boy too," I said. "So, what do you think about a junior?"

He beamed. "Really? You'd like that?"

"Why not?" I questioned. "I like the name Jim. I'd want to call him Jimmy, though."

"I like that," he said. "Jimmy Junior has a nice ring to it."

"Okay, but what if we have two boys?" I ask.

"First one out is junior," he said.

"Okay, but what do we name the other one?" I question.

He thought for a second. "Well, if we have two boys, I don't want the other one to feel left out with one of them being named after me."

"Should we name the second one after someone else in the family, then?" I asked, and he nodded. "What about your dad?" I asked.

He smiled and agreed.

"That was *way* too easy," I said. "We fought over Laurie's name."

"Boys are easy," Jim said. "Its' the girls that are always difficult."

"So, if we have one boy, it's Jimmy Junior, and if it's two it's going to be Jimmy Junior and Billy after you and Dad," I said. "But what if one of them is a girl?"

"Not this again," Jim said, laughing as we both recounted how we had gone back and forth over girl names with Laurie.

"Oh, geez," I giggled. "What if it's two girls? We'll never figure out names for them!"

Jim chuckled and pulled into our garage.

Truthfully, I was hoping for one boy and one girl. Paula's son, Danny, was a handful. I couldn't imagine twin boys once they reached that toddler age.

Kenny was sitting on our couch watching television when we entered. He jumped up and smiled. "She's asleep," he said. "Are you guys okay? Your mom called and told me what happened."

"We're fine," Jim said and disappeared into our bedroom. He seemed a little disgruntled – probably wondering just how much detail my mom had given Kenny. Knowing Mom, Kenny knew everything she did.

"Ugh, it's late," I moaned. "And, I have to take those pictures to Galigani tonight before I get to go to bed." I was already heading toward the kitchen where I'd left the envelope full of the incriminating photos. I wanted to get some sleep before I had to meet Galigani in the morning. Too bad he needed those pictures to review before his meeting with Sarah tomorrow morning, otherwise I would have just given them to him later.

"Hey, Kate, I'm meeting my friends for a late night jam session. Scotty lives near Galigani's office. You want me to drop them off for you?"

"You wouldn't mind?" I asked.

"Nah? I owe you anyway. I ordered an extra large pizza with the works, on your dime. I thought I'd leave you and Jim some leftovers, but I ate it all."

I laughed. "It's okay. I think Jim and I are going straight to bed. "I handed him the folder. "This has important information inside, okay? Make sure it gets to Galigani's mailbox."

"Will do," he said.

"You are a doll," I said, walking him out.

I was so anxious for bed, my skin itched. Despite the volatile night, I knew I needed my rest.

I changed into my pjs and practically dove under the covers next to Jim. And to be honest, I think I might have actually been asleep before my head hit the pillow.

Suddenly there was a knock on our door.

I bolted upright and looked at the clock. We'd only been in bed about an hour.

I grabbed my robe and hurried down the hallway to the answer the door. I was surprised to see Galigani standing there.

If he had been planning on stopping by, why in the world would he have had me come all the way to his office?

Then, I saw a police cruiser parked out in the street. Two, in fact. Alarms started going off in my head. "Hey, Kate," he said.

"Everything all right?" I asked.

"Yeah, for the most part, but I'm going to need some more copies of those pictures you took," he said.

Jim was by my side; I felt him touch my shoulder. "What's going on?" Jim asked.

Galigani frowned. "Your nanny got mugged out in front of my office."

"Kenny!" I yelped.

"He's fine," Galigani said, nodding toward Kenny's yard next door where I could see him standing and talking to his mom.

"Geez, hold on," I said, exiting the house and stepping out into the dark. I crossed over into Kenny's yard, and I was outraged when I saw the poor kid's face. "Kenny! What happened!"

His mom put her hands on her hips. "What in the world did you have my son delivering?" she questioned.

"Mom, don't be mad at Kate," Kenny said, defending me. His lip was busted, and his eyes were already starting to bruise.

"What happened? Who did this to you?" I cried and gave Kenny a big hug.

Guilt overwhelmed me.

This is my fault for sending him off in the middle of the night.

Kenny pulled back. "I'm fine, really," he said. "But, some creep jumped me in front of Galigani's office. He took the envelope you had given me. I'm sorry."

"It's okay," I said. "I have copies on my computer. I'm just glad you're okay. Who was it? A grown man?"

My blood was boiling.

Who punches a kid in the face like that?

"Did a grown man really punch you in the face?" I asked.

"Pretty much," he said. "Galigani was there, and he ran outside, and the guy took off. But, we're pretty sure it was that lumberjack, Raymond. The guy we took the photos of."

"What?" Kenny's mother demanded.

"I could have taken the pictures over for you," Jim said. "Why didn't you ask me?"

"I... I don't know, Kenny said he had a jam—a"

"I told Kate I would, okay? It's no big deal," Kenny said, interrupting me, and I got the distinct impression his mother didn't know about his late night rendezvous with his friends.

"I'm so, so sorry, Kenny," I said.

His mom huffed and squinted at her son, then she turned on a heel and went into the house. I was a little bit afraid of what awaited Kenny later.

How did Raymond even know that Kenny had those photos?

Kenny just wanted to go to bed; I couldn't blame him. He assured me again he didn't blame me for what happened, and after talking to the police, he headed inside.

The police questioned Galigani and me about what Kenny had been delivering, and they assured us that they would handle things.

After the police left, Galigani followed Jim and me into the house. "Please tell me you had additional copies of those?" Galigani asked.

I grabbed a flash drive from our home office and handed it to Galigani while we stood in the living room – all very upset about what had happened to Kenny. "Yeah, this pregnancy brain I've been dealing with didn't prevent me from making copies of the photos. Only problem is my office printer is out of ink."

"I'll get these printed before our meeting in the morning," Galigani said, sighing. "Poor kid. Maybe don't send him to drop off your paperwork for me anymore?"

"Agreed," I said, shaking my head. "I can't believe someone assaulted Kenny."

"Well, I'm furious," Jim said. "I thought this was a simple cheating husband case. It could have been Kate getting mugged!"

Galigani chewed his lip. He didn't want to debate with Jim the merits vs. dangers of the career I'd chosen.

"Don't worry, honey. I can handle myself," I said with more bravado in my voice than I felt. I turned to Galigani. "Did you see anything?'

"Not much. But, I'm pretty sure it was Raymond. He was tall with a beard. Anyway, who else would want those pictures but him?" Galigani questioned.

"Yeah," I said, "But how did he know we had the pictures? I didn't think he ever saw me."

"You're new at the PI game," Galigani said. "You're going to make mistakes."

I sighed. I didn't like hearing that. "I guess so," I said. "I feel like I've been making a lot of those lately."

"And, things are about to get a lot more complicated," Galigani said. "With Raymond's mistress dead, he's starting to look pretty suspicious for that extra case you've picked up. Now he attacked someone to get hold of the photographs. He probably knows his wife is about to find out about the affair. We're going to have to work with the police on this one because they're going to want those photographs."

"You should get some rest," Galigani said. "We have a busy day tomorrow." Galigani thanked me again for the thumb drive with the pictures, and headed out.

Jim and I locked up and then made our way back to our bedroom. Despite crawling back into bed, sleep eluded me.

I was wide awake. My mind was going off in a million different directions. I couldn't shut it down.

First, I reviewed everything we had for Sarah in the morning. Galigani had bugged Raymond's phone. We had text messages, emails, and entire phone conversations recorded that incriminated the man. He probably didn't realize we had all of that, in addition to those photographs I'd taken of him and Morgan.

Second, I was worried about the actual conversation. How was I supposed to tell a woman that her husband was cheating? Third, that her husband's mistress had been poisoned, automatically making him a suspect for murder – and probably her as well, if we're being honest.

It was a lot to think about. I just lay there, staring up at the ceiling. I heard Jim roll over, and I glanced in his direction to see him looking at me through tired eyes. "You all right, babe?"

Fourth – I was worried about Jim. Why had he lied to me? Well, not so much lie as just omit telling me something important, but still it felt like a lie. Why wouldn't he talk to me about what he and Cassandra had gotten into an argument about? It made me uncomfortable that he was so unwilling to talk to me about something, and that thought was going to keep me up for a good bit that night.

"I'm fine," I lied. "Go to sleep, honey."

He nodded, kissed my cheek, and then rolled over – exhausted. He was asleep in a matter of minutes.

How could he do that?

Just shut off his brain?

My brain never worked that way. It was at least an hour before I finally managed to drift off to sleep that night.

CHAPTER 8

*W*hen I awoke, Jim had already left for work. I scrambled to get dressed for my meeting with Galigani and take care of Laurie at the same time.

When would I learn that I actually need a sitter before I have to leave?

It seemed impossible to juggle Laurie's morning needs and even a cup of coffee, much less a shower and make-up.

By the time Kenny knocked on my front door, I only had one shoe on and was having a hard time wrestling my other shoe out of Laurie's hands.

My heart lurched to see his face. One eye was swollen shut, and his lips were about three times their normal size.

"Kenny! You poor thing," I grabbed his sweatshirt and pulled him into my house.

"Aw, don't worry, Kate. It looks a lot worse than it feels."

"You should go home and sleep. I'll call my mom to watch Laurie," I said, scrambling around the room looking for my cell phone.

He waved a hand at me as something plopped onto the floor in my living room. Laurie, who'd been sitting on her play mat, drooling on my dress shoe, happily dropped it in exchange for Kenny's hand.

With his free hand, Kenny passed me my discarded shoe.

I slipped the shoe on, saying. "So, who's Scotty and why doesn't your mom want you to hang out with him?"

A guilty smile crossed swollen lips. "He's butterfly's brother."

Kenny had recently been broken-hearted by a girl a few years older than him, a girl we'd nicknamed butterfly because of her tattoo.

"Ah," I said.

"I sent him a selfie; he showed butterfly, and she's going to make me chicken soup today."

"Oh my goodness, Kenny. Do I have to play mom now and tell you she's no good for you? Remember the last time you saw her she was with the guy with—"

He held up a hand. "I remember, Kate."

"But you don't want to listen. Kenny, take my advice. Once a cheater always a cheater!"

"Pfft," he said, dismissing me. "I don't want anything serious with her, Kate. I'm seventeen."

I laughed. "Okay, well, as long as you aren't planning a wedding. Look, I have to go meet with poor Lumberjack's wife. Who knows how many times the dirt bag cheated on her?"

Kenny was already grabbing the remote and flipping through cartoons, more for himself than Laurie who was now fascinated with my cell phone.

There it is!

I snatched it out of her hands, and she cried. Kenny scooped her up and moved to the couch.

I fired off a message to my mom, while I finished my hair and make-up.

Then as I flew out the door, I yelled to Kenny, "My mom will be here in about 30 minutes, so you can go get some rest. Drink lots of water today? Okay? It will help with the swelling."

I closed the door behind me, but still heard Kenny sing out, "Chicken soup is good for swelling too."

<><><>

ON THE DRIVE to Galigani's office, I contemplated the task ahead of us.

How do you look a woman in the eye and tell her that her suspicions about her sleazy husband are right?

By some miracle, I arrived on time to Galigani's. He'd instructed me to arrive about thirty minutes prior to when Sarah was scheduled. He said his female clients hiring him for things like this – cheating husbands or boyfriends – did one of three things. Showed up ridiculously early in anticipation of the news, showed up ridiculously late because they weren't too anxious to hear it, or pulled a no show because they decided they didn't want to know. Never, he said, did they show up on time. So, turns out, I didn't need to be there early. Sarah was a type two – she was late by nearly forty minutes which was just insane to me.

I couldn't imagine keeping someone waiting for that long, and especially if you're waiting to find out if your husband is cheating, well, I guess I'm a type one.

Upon arrival, Galigani poured me a cup of coffee and brought me up to speed.

"So kid, Morgan dying last night complicates our simple cheating husband case."

I nodded. "Do you know the cause of death?"

He shook his head. "Autopsy is scheduled today. But I can tell you, that if it's ruled a homicide, Raymond is going to be suspect numero uno, despite his not being near the theater last night."

"What about Kenny's assault?" I asked.

Galigani smile. "My security cam caught it on video."

"And? Is it Raymond?"

"It's blurry, but it certainly looks like it's him. I gave the tape to one of my police buddies last night. He said they're going to need Sarah to identify him, but he agreed to let us talk to her first."

"Right after hearing that her husband is a cheat, she probably won't hesitate to point out the creep, if it was him in the video," I said.

From Galigani's office window, we saw Sarah pull into the parking lot. I stood and opened the office door, before she even knocked.

Sarah was a petite blonde who looked ten years younger than she actually was. Her face looked like it had never gone through puberty – in other words, she looked like a little girl rather than a forty-year-old woman. I wish I was that youthful looking.

Galigani invited her to sit, and she anxiously came over and plopped down across from him.

I sat next to her, hoping she would feel some kind of sisterhood support by my closeness.

She smiled at me sadly, letting me know she appreciated my support.

"So, it's true then, isn't it? Ray is a two-timer?"

Galigani worked his lip, his large black mustache going haywire. He pulled out a manila envelope from his desk drawer and drummed his fingers on it.

Next to me, Sarah inhaled sharply, and I instantly reached for her hand.

She gripped my hand gratefully and nodded at the envelope as if she was ready for the contents to be revealed.

"Kate was able to get those photographs for you," Galigani said, as he slid the envelope across the desk. "I'm very sorry," he added.

Sarah's hands shook as she opened up the file and simply dumped the photographs out onto the desk. She spread them out. There were five. Morgan in her slinky negligee in Raymond's lap. A clear shot of Raymond's face as he embraced Morgan. And then a few of the couple that were... edgy, to say the least.

Sarah started crying, and I felt physically sick to my stomach. Before Galigani or I could offer any words of comfort, she spat out, "You know he hasn't been home in two days? Told me he was taking a guy's trip. He's probably off somewhere with that stupid bimbo! Well, good riddance! I'm filing for divorce *today!*" She wiped her face. "Who is this woman anyways? I've never seen her."

"Her name is Morgan," Galigani said. "And, you're saying you don't know her?"

"No, should I?" Sarah asked, still wiping her face while attempting to control her breathing. She looked both sad and furious—a whirlwind of emotions etched across her face.

Galigani opened his mouth to reply, but Sarah cut him off, "I should have known. I don't know why I'm shocked. I think this has been going on for months – maybe longer. First, you know, he just... stopped talking to me about things. He wasn't lying, not really, just not telling me stuff."

My heart lurched.

"Lying by omission," I said under my breath, thinking about how Jim failed to mention his little incident at the bakery.

"Exactly," Sarah said. "And, then, it just spiraled. I started catching him in lies. I found weird emails and text messages he would B.S. his way around. Then he started taking phone calls late at night – having to go to the office for unexpected reasons."

The thought of Jim's out of town trip last week sprang into my mind.

No, no!

Don't go there, Kate.

That was a business trip. I was sure of it.

"I shouldn't be so surprised," Sarah continued. "But you think you know a person... you think they would never hurt you. That they would be honest with you. That they would take their vows just as seriously as you do. But, no. He got tired of me and just... found someone new..."

My heart raced.

Would Jim ever get tired of me?

I think about all the baby weight I've already put on. About what my first pregnancy did to my body with Laurie – how much worse was it going to be with twins?

Would I ever get back to even remotely what I could consider normal?

Is Jim even still attracted to me?

I tried to brush those panicky thoughts away, but they were stuck in my head. Jim's decision not to tell me about his fight with

Cassandra really bothered me – more than I realized. I knew Jim was a good man; he would never stray, but sitting there listening to Sarah say the same things about that creep, Raymond, well, it did something to my head.

I brushed it away finally. It took me a good minute to get those thoughts out of my head, but I knew the man I married. I loved him, and I knew he loved me. I wouldn't let this crap get in my head and affect our relationship.

I refuse to go there!

"There is something else you should know, Sarah," Galigani said, turning his computer screen around to face her. "It's about Morgan, the woman your husband had been seeing."

Sarah huffed. "I really could care less about her. I hope he leaves her in a few years for someone younger. That's what she deserves."

That was bitter, but I couldn't blame her. Galigani cleared his throat. "That's going to be difficult. Sarah, Morgan is dead."

Sarah's eyes shot open, and she froze.

Hearing that the mistress was dead was confusing news. I could see it in her face. A part of her secretly glad. Almost like she'd gotten revenge without actually having to do anything. And then that other part, the part that was plastered all over her face, guilt for feeling that way.

"Dead?" Sarah asked. "How? Why? What happened?"

"The police are still investigating," Galigani said. "They asked me to share this video with you. It's from my security camera. It picked up a mugging that took place last night in front of my office. The victim was a teenage boy who happened to be carrying these photos of your husband." Galigani played the video.

Sarah's eyes widened. It was a fuzzy shot, but even I knew who it was. I had trailed that bald creep long enough to recognize his body type. I cringed. I wished Galigani had showed me the video beforehand because watching Kenny get beat up wasn't what I needed.

When I had left Laurie with him this morning, I had wanted to break down crying just seeing those bruises. He was a tough kid, but he was still just a teenager. A kid.

"That's Raymond!" she shrieked and started crying all over again. "Why would he attack that boy?"

"Like I said, he stole our first copies of these pictures, but we had a backup," Galigani said. "We believe he might have caught on to Kate – that he realized Ms. Kate had taken pictures of him and Ms. Morgan."

"And, now Morgan is dead?" Sarah questioned, and she became pale. "You think my Raymond killed her? No, that's not right. I know he cheated... but... no, I don't think he would... he's not that type of person."

I was surprised she was defending him. I supposed she must still love him even though she was planning to leave him.

"I understand," Galigani said. "But, he did hurt this boy."

"Yes," Sarah said. "That was definitely him... I can't believe Raymond would beat up a kid! That's not like him. He's not a violent person."

"Is it possible, Sarah, that Raymond believes if he covers up what happened with Morgan he could save his marriage? Would he be willing to kill her to keep you?" Galigani asked.

"Well, it's too late for that, isn't it?" Sarah hissed. "First I find out that he cheats and beats up a kid, and now he is a suspect in a murder case?"

"It's not murder yet," I said.

She glared at me.

"I...well, what I mean is we're waiting to hear the cause of death," I said lamely.

Sarah stiffened. "I'm not sticking around to find out. I'm done. I'm going straight to a lawyer when I leave here, and since he's apparently the type of man who batters kids, I should probably see if I can have an officer come to the house to help me gather my things in case that lunatic comes home!" She slammed her fists down. "I just... I just cannot believe any of this! I can't believe this is happening!"

"If Raymond reaches out to you, Sarah, would you please contact one of us, or better yet, contact the police?" Galigani asked.

"Believe me, I will," she said.

"Before you leave, Sarah, can I get you to write down your statement regarding the video that you do indeed believe that the man who assaulted young Kenneth was in fact your husband?" Galigani asked, presenting her with paper and pen.

"It would be my pleasure, Mr. Galigani," she said and scribbled her statement down with angry tears streaming down her face. "And, believe me, sir, as soon as I see Raymond, I'm calling the police!" She dug into her purse, pulling out her checkbook. She wrote down her final payment and handed it to Galigani. "You were worth every penny!"

She looked at me. "Thank you for the pictures. Would you please email some to me? I'd like to show them to my lawyer. And, I want to have them blown up really big. I'm going to put one up on the billboard down the street from his parent's house so they can see whose fault this divorce is without me having to talk to them."

I couldn't help it. I snickered. Galigani frowned at me.

Her idea was cold, but I kind of loved it. I wiped the smile from my face and said, "Of course, Sarah," I said, trying to maintain an air of professionalism.

But come on, a billboard down the street from his parent's house? That's hilarious.

A small smile broke across her face. "My husband's boss drives by that billboard every day on *her* way into work. Her husband cheated on her two years ago. I'm sure she'll have a few words to say to the man when she sees it."

At this, Galigani chuckled.

"I'll send them right over, Sarah," I said.

She stood up after signing her statement. She told us to forward her information to the police; she was more than happy to cooperate in the investigation.

"Sarah, my services have been retained by Cassandra's Cookies," I said, quickly filling her in on the details of how Cassandra had also collapsed at the party. "If I have any questions during my investigation, may I contact you?"

"Absolutely!" she said turning toward the door and waving goodbye.

Sarah left, with a bit more confidence in her step.

She had a plan to keep herself afloat after the devastating news – a revengeful one, but at least she wasn't curled up in a ball letting the news get the better of her.

I was proud of her.

"That wasn't as bad as I thought it would be," I said to Galigani once Sarah was gone.

"You see all types of reactions after you have been at this for a while," Galigani said. "Unfortunately in the PI business, cheating spouse is the most common type of case you're going to get. Well, cheating everything, really you should hear some of the stuff business partners do to each other. Especially, starting out. Unlike you, it took me years before I got something like a murder case to go on. When you branch out and start your own practice, this is the type of stuff you can expect."

"It sure isn't pretty," I said. "But, at least Sarah handled it well. For my first infidelity case, I suppose it could have been a lot worse."

"You have no idea," Galigani said. "One woman, early in my career, was convinced I had Photoshopped the pictures and broke a lamp in my office."

"Are you serious?"

"Dead serious," Galigani said. "She eventually came around, though. She even bought me a new lamp." He pointed to the standing lamp in the corner. "It was her apology gift for overreacting. But, I really didn't blame her. She didn't want to believe it. I know I wouldn't have wanted to hear it."

"Same here," I said.

And then without wanting to, my mind went to Jim.

Had he really been out of town last weekend with a client?

CHAPTER 9

*I*t was just one of those nights. One of those nights where no matter how hard you try, you just cannot get to sleep. Where your brain is running a million miles an hour – thinking about the next day's to-do list, everything you didn't get done that day, finances, babies, health, your marriage, and all things that could possibly keep you up late worrying. The thing that was most prominent on my mind that night?

Sarah.

There was just so much about our conversation that bothered me. For one, she had been so blindsided by Raymond's betrayal. That was probably what pestered me the most about it – she hadn't really expected. Sure, she had had her suspicions, but clearly, a part of her was expecting Galigani and me to tell her she was just being paranoid; that her suspicions were incorrect and unfounded.

But, that's not what happened. She was shocked. And, the first thing that Sarah said she noticed that was off? Raymond stopped talking to her about everything which eventually led into him keeping more and more secrets.

I glanced over to Jim who was fast asleep beside me. His nose was

scrunched up slightly, his face pressing into his pillow. He looked so...
so... relaxed.

Yet, here I was trying my hardest not to have a complete and total
panic attack over one single decision of his to just not tell me something. And, he was acting like it was nothing. Like he had hadn't just
planted some seed in my head.Deciding that there was just no way I
was going to get any sleep that night, I slipped out of bed. I've never
been the type of person who enjoys wasting time. If I wasn't getting
any sleep or legitimate rest, I wasn't just going to stare up into the
dark at my bedroom ceiling. I was going to get some work done.

I headed down the hall and slipped into our home office, sitting
down at our desk and pulling out my laptop. Despite Jim's reserva-
tions about his incident with Cassandra, I knew I had to look into it.
Cassandra was one of the victims, and she'd been the one to hire me
to begin with. Even though I most certainly didn't suspect my
husband's involvement, I still needed to stay caught up with the
police.

In short, I needed to know what had happened whether Jim
wanted to tell me or not.

I felt a little funny going behind his back, but I needed to talk to
Cassandra anyway. A quick Google search, and I found her email on
the *Cassandra's Cookies* website.

I sent her a quick note, asking if there was an appropriate time we
could get together to chat, and that I had some questions regarding
the case she'd hired me to solve.

While figuring out tomorrow's meal plan online, I saw an email
notification.

Cassandra had responded.

At first, I was surprised to get such a prompt response at five in the
morning, but I quickly noted in her email that she was still staying in
the hospital. The woman was just as wide awake as I was at the
moment.

I'd been in the hospital my fair share of times, and I'd never been
able to get any quality sleep there. She was probably sitting there,
playing on her phone when my email had popped up.

She told me I could come by the hospital anytime because the doctor said she probably wouldn't be dismissed until late afternoon the following day.

Just as I was about to close my laptop to start getting ready for a quick trip to the hospital, I noted Cassandra's sign off. "Come by anytime – Cassandra Sanders," she had written, and alarms started going off in my head.

"Cassandra Sanders..." I said under my breath. I hadn't realized what her full name was.

But honestly, what could I have been thinking—that it was cookies?

"Cassandra Sanders," I said again. There was something familiar about the name. I closed my laptop and stood up, concentrating for a moment. I headed over to a bookshelf and plucked one of Jim's old high school yearbooks off one of the shelves.

After just a few moments of flipping through the book, I found the Junior's Top Dogs page – basically all those best laughs, most likely to succeed.

And, there was Cassandra Sanders standing next to my Jim – "Couple most likely to get married."

Anger flared in my chest, and I slammed the yearbook shut.

There was no denying the fact that the girl in the picture was the same woman I'd met as Cassandra. The flaming red hair of hers was a dead giveaway.

I was livid. Not only did Jim keep the fact that the police had been called on him a secret – but he had failed to mention that the bakery belonged to his high school girlfriend!

I'd never met her, obviously, and Jim really didn't talk about her too much. He had mentioned dating a Cassandra girl back in the day, but I didn't realize she still lived in San Francisco. And I certainly didn't know that she was the one making me those brownies he oh-so willingly kept running out to get me.

Why hadn't he told me?

Unless, he had something to hide?

I was definitely going to the hospital to speak to her now. If I left now I could be home before Jim even woke up. Just in case, I left him a note stating that I hadn't been able to sleep and was going to take care of something work related.

I was vague in my note, but I figured there was a good chance he could guess who I was heading off to talk to. He probably wouldn't be thrilled to wake up to that note, but I didn't care. I needed answers not just for work but for my own peace of mind.

I set Laurie's monitor next to Jim's nightstand before getting dressed and heading out.

I sent another email to Cassandra, asking if it was okay if I dropped by in thirty minutes. Her response was an emphatic 'yes' followed by her hospital room number.

Once I got in my car, I texted Kenny to come over as soon as he was up just in case I was late getting home. I didn't want to make Jim late for work watching Laurie.

Then I messaged Cassandra that I was on the way and dropped my phone in the passenger seat.

My mind was still all over the place. I was literally on my way to talk to my husband's high school girlfriend – an old girlfriend he'd failed to mention he had obviously been talking to.

Jim never kept secrets from me.

I didn't like it one bit.

Why hadn't he said anything to me?

I'm pretty sure I was white-knuckling my steering wheel the entire way to the hospital. I was mad at Jim. Mostly hurt. And, I kept thinking about Sarah. About how blindsided she'd been.

My phone beeped again when I arrived in the parking lot at the hospital. It was an email from Galigani. The autopsy report for Morgan had been sent his way by his buddy at the local station, and Galigani had been kind enough to forward it to me.

I liked that he was willing to call his contact for me, but I knew I was eventually going to have to make some contacts of my own. I read through the report. Morgan had been poisoned via chloroform.

The chloroform had been in some brownies that Cassandra's shop had made – the ones coated in bright orange icing.

Oh my goodness!

Good thing it wasn't the purple icing, I thought.

Either way, I'd had some sort of aversion to the purple brownies that night, so it's not like I would have been poisoned. That stuff made it in the trash can quick.

But, I was glad I'd gotten that email from Galigani. That way, I had some information before I spoke with Cassandra. I headed into the hospital, and eventually found my way to her room.

She was sitting up in bed, hooked up to an IV. She looked well enough, thankfully. Probably just waiting for some of the chloroform to get out of her system.

"Kate," she said and smiled at me. "How is the case going?"

"Well I do have some information. I know Morgan was having an affair with a married man. Do you know anything about that?"

"I knew she was dating a guy named Raymond," Cassandra said as I made my way over. I pulled up a chair beside her hospital bed and pulled out the notebook I'd snagged from the house so I could take notes.

"That would be him," I said.

"Yeah, he seemed kind of... sketchy," Cassandra said. "But, I only met him once or twice. He would swing by the bakery every once in a while, and drop off some lunch for her. He picked her up for a date once. He seemed a little old for her, but she was kind of into that. She wanted a sugar daddy type thing."

"So obviously, I'm looking into Raymond. But, he was nowhere near the theater when Morgan was killed," I said.

"Yeah," Cassandra said. "But, when I talked to my doctors and the police, they told me someone poisoned my brownies. I know Morgan and I both ate some. Raymond doesn't have a key to the bakery or anything, but maybe he could have... I don't know..."

"Would Morgan have let him into the back?" I asked.

"I guess she could have," Cassandra said. "But, I don't know why she would do that. I don't let anyone into the back who isn't a baker. Our cashiers aren't even allowed back there. You know, I need to keep the kitchen hygienic. And Morgan had been working there for a while. She knew the rules."

It was interesting that Cassandra had brought up the poisoned brownies. I'd been wondering how to broach the subject, thinking she might get defensive of her employees. But it didn't seem like she was trying to hide anything.

"I need to ask about the incident between you and my husband," I said, changing subjects. I once again decided to feel her out. Not let her know what I already knew just to see if she would be honest with me.

She rolled her eyes. "It was stupid, really."

"I need to hear your side of things," I said.

She sighed. "Well, if I'm being honest, I'm not sure if Jim told you, but we dated briefly way back in high school."

"Yeah, he told me," I said even though he hadn't exactly. At least not recently.

She nodded. "Jim had come in a few times getting those brownies for you," Cassandra said. "He didn't recognize me at first. It was probably about the second or third time, and I finally said something to him. Just told him who I was, thought we would have a good laugh about it – maybe chat about old times and see what each other had been up to since high school. That sort of thing. Well, he looks me up and down and makes this awful comment about how he had obviously *dodged a bullet.*"

I frowned. "Oh?"

"Yeah," she said, a very annoyed pout on her face. "And, frankly, I didn't care for what he said to me. I thought it was just so rude. I mean, we were kids when we dated, but I remembered ending on good terms, you know? I can't imagine what I could have done for him to say that to me. It was just so mean and spiteful, and I probably overreacted. I snapped at him, he snapped back, and it just escalated, and I finally just called the police to end it."

I really didn't want to believe a word she had just said to me. I couldn't imagine Jim making a comment like that to someone.

He was just so... sweet.

KILLER CRAVINGS

She must have guessed that I didn't believe her because she sat upright and looked at me. "It surprised me too," she said. "Like I said, we dated back in high school. He was always such a gentleman. He was nice to women. Nice to everybody. To hear that come out of his mouth about me, well, it set me off. And, honestly, I'm sorry for my part in it. I overreacted, but that doesn't mean it didn't hurt my feelings."

I still wasn't sure. I couldn't imagine Jim making a comment like that to her face. But, I tried not to let her know I didn't believe her.

"Well, I'm very sorry to hear that," I said. "But, thank you for talking with me. Is there anything else you can tell me about Morgan that might lead me in the right direction?" I asked.

"I don't know," Cassandra admitted. "She kept to herself. We weren't particularly close. She came into work and then headed off. She dated a lot, though. Raymond was just the latest of the older men she dated. I couldn't tell you their names, though. Like I said, she wanted to find herself a sugar daddy. She didn't like to work, but she was willing to do it until she found what she wanted in a guy. A guy with deep pockets."

"Thank you, Cassandra," I said, getting up from my seat.

I was very frustrated, but I tried my best not to show it. Cassandra thanked me again for looking into the case for her. She expressed her sympathy for what happened to Morgan, and admitted she was very worried about her business after having an employee killed by someone poisoning her brownies.

She gave me a list of employees and anyone who would have access to the bakery for one reason or another.

I headed out, my mind swimming once again. The fact that Jim didn't tell me Cassandra was his ex-girlfriend was really bothering me.

And, honestly, she was very pretty. Model pretty, not mommy pretty…

I was… pregnant with babies number two and three.

Laurie had certainly changed the way I looked – and this pregnancy was only going to do that even more.

Was Jim still attracted to me?

Had he been going to the bakery to fantasize about an ex-girlfriend?

Was there something even more going on than that?

I couldn't think about it. It was making sick. Why wouldn't Jim talk to me?

Was Jim... was Jim cheating on me?

CHAPTER 10

*W*hen I left the hospital, my frustrations were at an all time high.

I knew my husband.

I knew him well.

We'd dated for a long time before we married, and we'd been married for a almost four years now. Plus, we had a good, healthy marriage.

Or, at least, I believed we did...

Jim was a nice, wonderful man. He was friendly. Loving. Caring. Smart. Funny. I loved him. He was not only my husband, but my best friend.

And yet...

I just couldn't shake this feeling that something about this situation was wrong. First, he failed to mention to me about the police being called. Now, it turned out, the woman who'd called the police on him was an ex-girlfriend.

And, according to her, he had made some rude comment to her. That just didn't sound like Jim.

Was Cassandra lying?

Had the two of them been seeing each other and got into some sort of spat?

I wasn't sure what to think. I know one thing: I was very distracted on my drive home. Not that that would have mattered.

It was dark, only a hint of light coming up from the distant horizon. A slight blush color covered half the sky while behind me it was still pitch black – stars still in the sky, and the moon only a sliver. It was a lovely juxtaposition that I really couldn't appreciate with everything that was running through my mind.

As I drove through an intersection, a flicker of light caught my eye. I saw the headlights, and I could hear the spinning of tires.

My breath caught and I swerved.

The car barreling toward me turned also—but not to get out of my way. Instead, they were swerving toward me as if to ensure they hit me.

My heart lurched, and I braced for impact. The car hit the back driver's side door, t-boning my car. My vehicle began to spin. The steering wheel jerked so abruptly that I had to throw my hands up to prevent my wrists from being jerked about. I felt the airbag smash into my face, and my mouth filling with blood.

I was only vaguely aware that my car was flipping. I could see out my cracked window as the ground appeared to swoosh overhead. At last, my car came to a grinding halt as my vehicle slid off the road and into a parking meter. My back bumper crunched, and once I was at last still I took a deep breath.

I'm alive, right?

I touched my head, wiggled my toes, and checked over my arms. I knew when adrenaline was pumping, it could be difficult to ascertain if anything was broken or injured, so I remained fairly still until I could get my bearings together.

And oh no.

My babies!

I glanced up, and I saw the car. A red Toyota Takoma with a bent fender. My entire body tensed, and I watched the vehicle bail. It drove away, tires shrieking. Down the street, red flashing police lights erupted, and I felt an instant sense of relief knowing that someone of authority had seen the accident.

Accident?

It was no accident. Raymond drove a Toyota Takoma with a bent fender. I'd recognized his truck as soon as my car stopped spinning. I'd been trailing the guy for over a month. I knew who he was. I knew what he drove. I could have spotted that truck a mile away.

I stayed in my car, and I didn't bother moving to search for my phone since a cop was already on the way. Being pregnant, I didn't want to risk anything. I was already worried enough about my twin babies after being told I'd a higher chance of a miscarriage after the carbon monoxide poisoning incident.

Less than two minutes went by, and then a flashlight shined in my eye. "Miss, are you all right?" he asked, and I could see him peering in the back seat.

"Car seat is empty," I said, thankful for my baby on board sticker. "Little one is at home with dad."

"Okay, good," he said. "I just wanted to make sure. Ma'am, how is your neck? Is anything hurting?"

"No, I think I'm okay, but I'm pregnant. Can you please call for an ambulance? I'd rather be safe than sorry," I said. "And, I know who hit me. His name is Raymond Kent. I'm a PI, and his wife hired me to investigate him. I think he was trying to kill me."

"Do you know—"

"License plate? Yup, I have it memorized," I hissed.

The officer smirked at me slightly – like he was proud of me, this complete stranger, for being so prepared. He called for an ambulance, put out a search for Raymond, and then came and waited by the car with me.

"I'm definitely pressing charges against this creep," I told the cop.

"You should," he agreed. "I'm happy to take your statement as soon as you get cleared by the medics."

The paramedics arrived almost immediately, but even so, I was already starting to feel really achy. I hoped nothing was broken, but I was pretty sure that I was going to at least be experiencing some whiplash.

They put me on a stretcher, and when it was raised up, I could see just how destroyed my car was. I gritted my teeth. I'd definitely seen Raymond's car – and I was pretty sure he had been driving. That bearded face of his was a dead giveaway.

The paramedics spoke calmly to me like I was having some sort of panic attack, but I was more angry than frightened. It could have been a lot worse. It took less than ten minutes to get me to the hospital, and I was taken straight back to the ER.

Since I was pregnant, they didn't do any x-rays, especially since I wasn't complaining too seriously except for what I'm sure would be a good bit of bruising. They then took me to get an ultrasound with the on-call gynecologist where they checked over my babies – mostly to check for any signs of placental abruption. Thankfully, the babies were fine, and so was I apart from a small line of stitches I had to get in my right eyebrow – thanks to the airbag.

I'd asked the doctor to call Jim when I'd first arrived, but since Jim was already listed as my emergency contact, he had already been called. I assumed he would be there sooner or later, but I was starting to get anxious. They put me in a room while my doctor filled out some discharge paperwork, and that's when Jim finally arrived.

The man entered my hospital room, eyes blazing. "Kate!" he yelped, hurrying inside. He sat on the edge of the hospital bed and touched my face. My face was a bit bruised from the airbag, and I'm sure the fresh stitches made it look worse than it actually was. He looked completely panicked and shaky. I couldn't believe that just an hour before I was stewing in the car wondering if this man could possibly be cheating on me.

Maybe I could blame it on pregnancy hormones – I was acting nuts.

"I'm fine, Jim," I assured him and smiled. "Where's Laurie?"

"She's with Kenny," he said. "I'm so glad you're all right. When they called me, I freaked out. They said your car was totaled and that it had been a hit and run?"

"Yeah, but I was able to ID the driver. It was Creepy Raymond," I said.

"The same guy who beat up Kenny?" Jim questioned. "I'm going to kill him."

"You can't kill him," I said, groaning slightly. "Then you'd be in jail, and my babies need their daddy."

All the thoughts I'd been entertaining about Jim's possible infidelity suddenly collided in my mind, and tears streamed down my face.

Jim squeezed my hand, and panic clouded his features. "Babe! Does something hurt? Should I call the doctor?"

I shook my head. "I'm fine. My hormones are out of whack. They're making me all emotional and irrational."

"Nah, you're always that way," he joked.

I dropped his hand. "That's not funny."

He stroked my hair. "I'm kidding." His phone vibrated in his pocket, and he pulled it out to glance at it. "Hey, your mom just texted me that she's here. I called her on my way to let her know you'd been in an accident." He set his phone down on the small table beside the hospital bed, and leaned in to kiss my forehead. "I'll grab her from the ER waiting room so she doesn't get lost."

"Thanks," I said to him, trying to actually sound thankful instead of flustered. Despite how sweet and worried he was acting, I was still a little annoyed with him. I wouldn't have felt the need to run out to the hospital if he'd just been straight with me about what had happened between him and Cassandra.

Maybe a tiny part of me is blaming him for what happened.

Normally, I'd never think that.

It wasn't Jim's fault I was running out to talk to Cassandra, and it wasn't Jim's fault that Raymond had decided to go after me.

None of it was Jim's fault, yet somehow my brain was trying to encourage me to find something to be angry with him about. It was that nagging feeling in the back of my head – that feeling that *something* just wasn't right.

I watched Jim leave; he hurried out of the room to go meet Mom. My mom had a tendency to wander and get distracted easily, so it was definitely necessary to escort her. She was the type of woman who could inadvertently start talking to a stranger and have a cruise to the Bahamas' booked by the time she made it to my room.

I leaned my head back, taking a moment to gather my bearings before my mom came in and started fussing over me. I smirked slightly, imagining that one day Laurie would moan and groan about how I needed to calm down and stop worrying about her.

Like my mom, I knew I never would. Funny how you realize that sort of thing once you become a parent.

Just as I was starting to relax a bit, something caught my eye.

Jim had left his phone.

There it was. Just sitting there within arm's reach. My mind raced back to my meeting with Sarah and Galigani. She'd said that the first thing she noticed was how Raymond had started omitting things... like what Jim was doing with the incident with Cassandra.

The second thing she'd said was that he had started getting strange emails and phones calls...

Every neuron in my brain was telling me to leave it alone. To trust my husband. To not reach over there and start going through his phone.

But, I didn't listen.

I snagged his phone. I don't know what I was looking for, but I was looking for something. I checked first to see if he was logged into his email, but he wasn't. I didn't know Jim's password for his email. I never really had a reason to go snooping through his emails before. I checked his messages. The first few texts that showed up were from me, Kenny, Mom, and a few guys from work. Okay, so he had least hadn't been contacting anyone recently.

Then it occurred to me that Cassandra had given me her number. Had Jim tried calling her? I typed her number into his phone to see if anything came up.

It did.

My breath caught.

He had her contact – her personal cell number – saved in his phone.

Not under her name, of course, but under the contact *Bakery*. I tried not to panic. I'd been having Jim go out for brownies for me quite often. It was certainly possible that Jim had asked for her number so he could call her whenever his wife, me, was having one of her pregnancy cravings.

But... why would Cassandra give him her cell number? Why not her work number?

My throat felt dry. My finger lingered over the contact number. It would be so easy to look and see if they had been messaging back and forth. My palms were sweaty.

It was this weird, ominous moment. If I clicked that name, it meant I didn't trust Jim. But, if I chose not to check, would I wind up being the fool later on?

I clicked it.

And, my stomach dropped when I saw a picture of Cassandra pop up on his cell in their message history. It wasn't anything too provocative. It was from over two weeks ago – probably right before the incident where Jim and she had gotten into it.

She was smiling in the little selfie, and her loose fitting tank top showed off a bra strap that made me want to go upstairs and find the room where she was staying just so I could smack her. The text read simply: *like the new haircut?*

I breathed deeply and told myself not to freak out just yet. It was a fairly innocent picture, and Jim hadn't even responded to it. I scrolled down. A text from Jim: *headed that way.*

Okay, that could be him saying he was coming to pick up brownies, right? Or, it could be something else...

Then I saw a few texts from Cassandra to Jim – just a bunch of smiley face and winky face emojis. That made my toes curl. I'm all for platonic male/female friendships, but why in the world was this woman sending stuff like that to Jim?

To my husband!

That wasn't appropriate. Then, I read something that I most definitely couldn't write off as nothing. A text from Cassandra: *Hey Sexy!!! You coming by later? ;)*

I think if I'd squeezed his phone any harder it would have shattered. But, I didn't have time to investigate further. I heard the door to my hospital room squeak, so I rushed to put the phone back down where I'd snatched it from.

Sexy!

Okay, if I'd not just been beaned by a car and wasn't completely sore, there was a good chance I would have marched right up to Cassandra's room and pulled her hair out.

My pregnancy was making me *just* crazy enough to want to push her out of the hospital's second floor window. I swear, I was ready to claw her eyes out – and, frankly, I wanted to start a screaming match with Jim.

But, I stopped myself as Jim and my mom entered the hospital room. I was training to be a PI. And, there was one thing Galigani had definitely hammered into me.

Never jump to conclusions.

Jim and I had a great marriage. I wasn't about to let my pregnancy brain get me all riled up. I wasn't going to scream and shout accusations.

Not yet.

And, frankly, I think I was a lot like Sarah. Like, billboard in front of your parents' house Sarah. If Jim was or had really already cheated on me, I was going to make sure I had evidence.

But most importantly, I love Jim.

I loved him so much even in that moment when I was fighting mad. I wasn't going to let myself believe he would ever cheat on me – not unless I had cold, hard evidence.

"My baby!" my mom yelped as she hurried over to me. "Are you okay? Jim told me one of your client's husbands did this to you!"

"I'm fine, Mom," I said and smiled at her. I even smiled at Jim as he sat down in one of the empty chairs in the room with that concerned look he often wore for me. I knew I had a good man there, so it really pained me knowing that I was about to turn our marriage into a case to be investigated.

CHAPTER 11

s I was finally getting discharged from the hospital, Galigani made an appearance. A nurse wheeled me out the front door, Jim and Mom walking alongside us. Galigani was standing out front, he never stepped foot in a hospital if he could avoid it.

He waved when he saw us. "You all right, Kate?"

"I'm fine," I said. "Glad to be alive. And my babies are alright, which is the main thing, and I'm annoyed about my car."

"I just got a call from the station. They arrested our good buddy Raymond," Galigani said.

"Good!" Jim hissed.

"Easy, big guy," Galigani said. "Kate, how are you feeling?" He gave me a sideways glance.

I squinted back at him, not sure what to expect. "Uh... Not bad considering, but I'm sure tomorrow when the pain meds wear off, I'll feel like a car hit me because, guess what? One did."

Galigani nodded. "Well, I want to give you a little sleuthing advice if you're up for hearing it."

"I could always use advice," I said, and Jim rolled his eyes and told me he'd pull the car around.

I watched him hurry off, and I sighed. I was trying really hard not to let this whole thing with Cassandra get to me. I was trying to be professional, but it was hard. Galigani put an arm across my mom's shoulder while we waited for Jim.

"You need to talk to Raymond," Galigani said. "Feel him out and see if you can get a confession out of him. Right now, it's not looking good for him – he seems like a pretty obvious suspect at the moment."

"Yeah, but the police have him," I said. "Oh, are you going to let me use one of your contacts?"

"Nope," Galigani said, and I frowned. "Kate, your goal is to one day start your own practice, correct?"

"Right..." I said, unsure of where he was going.

"That means, dear, you need to learn how to make nice with the police for yourself," he said. "It's better to work with them than against them."

I frowned, thinking of Inspector McNearny. He couldn't stand me, and knowing my luck, I was pretty sure he'd be at the station. He'd do everything in his power to keep me from speaking to Raymond. "What about McNearny?" I questioned.

"Forget about McNearny," he said. "He's not going to do you any favors."

"So then what am I supposed to do?" I asked. "Can you put in a good word with him—"

"Like I said, forget about him," Galigani said. "I'm training you, remember? And, I'm telling you, forget McNearny. You have got to, well, make some friends! Cops. That's how you get ahead in the business. Connections. Connections are important, and right now, you don't have any."

"Are you really pulling a sink or swim moment with my daughter?" Mom asked.

"Pretty much," he said. "If you start sinking, you know I'll help pull you up, Kate, but I want you to give this a go without borrowing my connections. Go to the station. Find a way to talk to Raymond."

"If you say so," I said under my breath as Jim pulled up with the car. He helped me out of the wheelchair, being as sweet as he could be. He probably would have let me fall over if he knew just how crazy my thoughts about him were in that moment. I really can't believe how much I'd let this whole thing get into my head. "I'll go by there later. I think I'm going to go home and rest for a little bit first."

"Good idea," Galigani said. "You did just get hit by a car."

I moaned, and said goodbye to Mom and Galigani. Jim drove me out of the hospital parking lot while I sulked in the passenger seat. We pulled into a car rental place, and I was glad to have that taken care of by the time we got home.

Kenny was sitting with Laurie in the living room. He was singing and making funny voices using a frog hand puppet to dance for her and she was giggling away.

"Kate," he said, standing up. "Are you all right? Jim told me what happened."

"I've been better," I said, plopping down on the couch.

Kenny got a good look at me and sighed. "You and I have matching black eyes from the same creep... yours looks a lot worse."

"She did get stitches," Jim said. "I have to get to work. Kenny, would you mind hanging around for a little bit longer? I think Kate could use the rest."

"I'm here so long as you need me," Kenny said, and I thanked him.

I took Laurie to her room and spent some time breastfeeding her before handing her off to Kenny again. I needed a nap, and I collapsed in my bed. I had no trouble falling asleep despite the aches and pains from the accident. When I woke up a couple hours later, I was surprised that I wasn't totally incapacitated from my injuries.

In fact, I felt refreshed. I picked up my phone to check the time, it was still pretty early in the afternoon. I also had a text from Paula; she wanted to do a girl's night, and honestly that sounded just lovely after the sort of week I'd had. Jim had already left, and Kenny had gotten Laurie down for a nap by the time I made it into the living room, Kenny was glued to his phone, texting and facetiming his friends.

"Butterfly?" I asked.

He smiled, "Nope. A sage woman told me; once a cheater, always a cheater. I'm chatting with French Fry."

I laughed. "Should I even ask?"

"I met her last night at the café around the corner. We split an order of fries. She's thinks I'm a big tough guy 'cuz I have a black eye."

"Oh my goodness, Kenny. You're jumping from the frying pan to the fire. You can't let this girl think you're someone you're not."

He frowned. "I'm not a big tough guy?"

We both burst out laughing.

"Listen, I have to go to the police station," Kate said. "Can you stay a while longer? Or should I call my mom?"

He shrugged. "It's no problem. French Fry is working today, so we're going to hang out later tonight, no worries," he said and smiled at me.

I thanked him and snagged a power bar from the kitchen before heading out. I was starving. I got into my stupid little rental car, griping and thinking about insurance claims and wondering how that was going to work – it was attempted vehicular homicide. Pretty sure that would make Raymond responsible for replacing my vehicle.

But this was my second accident, since Laurie had been born and I wondered if that meant my insurance was about to go.

I'd felt pretty confident up until the moment I arrived at the station. I saw McNearny heading inside, and I suddenly wished that I'd come a lot earlier.

"I shouldn't have taken that nap – I would have missed him," I groaned.

But, I had a job to do, so I sucked it up and headed inside. McNearny spotted me immediately, of course.

"Oh, geez, what are you doing here?" he groaned as I made my way into the station. "What happened to your face?"

"I was in an accident," I said, frowning. "Thanks for your concern."

"What can I help you with today?" he asked, sounding smug. It was hard to believe this was Galigani's former partner.

"I need to speak with someone you have in custody," I said. "Raymond Kent."

"Why in the world would I let you speak with someone we have in custody?" he questioned

I frowned. "Well, McNearny, I see that you're a little late getting

89

here, so I'm going to lay it out for you. The whole reason Raymond is in your jail cell is because he tried to kill me this morning." I pointed at the stitches above my brow. "He hit me with his truck – totaled my car. I need to speak to Raymond because, in addition to going after me, he's a suspect in a case I'm working. Now, are you going to play nice, or are you going to continue wasting my time?"

"Well, what do you think?" he smirked.

"Oh, leave her alone, Mac," a voice behind me said.

I turned around to see a woman in uniform giving McNearny this you-are-such-an-embarrassment look. "Why do you always insist on giving everyone such a headache?"

I smiled at her, but she just sort of shrugged in my direction. From what I gathered, the only reason she'd come to my defense was because McNearny was a mutual enemy. "Can it, Fisher," he said. "This is none of your business."

"Um, actually, Raymond is my perp, so..." she rolled her eyes and then looked at me. "Why do you want to talk to him?"

"I'm investigating him," I said. "I'm a Private Investigator, and I was looking into his extramarital affairs, and his side girl wound up dead. Then he went after me and my nanny, so, frankly, I think it's about time I had a face to face with the lumberjack."

"Lumberjack? Ha! That's funny. That's exactly what I thought of him too." She turned to McNearny. "I like her," she said, and McNearny rolled his eyes.

"Do what you want," he snarled and stormed off.

She stepped toward me and put out her hand. "Officer Deb Fisher. I was the one who snagged Raymond trying to get out of town this morning. You were the woman he hit? Kate?"

I shook her hand. "That would be me," I said.

"Sure did piss him off, huh?"

"Raymond or McNearny?"

She laughed again. "Funny. I like that."

"Listen, I know it's probably not protocol, but I need to speak with Raymond. It's for my case."

Deb stroked her chin; she seemed to be contemplating my request.

"You think you can get him to state he was trying to kill you?" Deb asked.

"I can try."

"The lack of confidence in your tone isn't convincing me to let you into an interrogation room with him, hon," she said, removing her cap to place it on the front counter at the station so that she could redo her chestnut brown bun that had started to fall loose.

"I can do it," I said.

"Atta girl," she said, and I swear she sort of winked at me.

What an odd character.

But I liked her anyway.

I followed her into the back of the station, and looked at Raymond through a two-way mirror. It made my skin crawl. He was a big, intimidating guy. I hadn't really seen him up close before; I was glad he was handcuffed.

"You ready?" Deb asked, and I nodded.

She let me into the room, and I closed the door behind me. Raymond sat upright when he saw me, and a scowl appeared on his face. "You got to be kidding me," he said. "You're a cop?"

I didn't answer.

He leaned back in his chair.

I sat across from him, and just stared at him with what had to be the most pissed off face he had ever seen. He didn't like the silence. He started tapping on the table. I waited just long enough until the quiet made us both a little uncomfortable.

"I'm pregnant." I hissed at him, and I could tell this bothered him.

"Oh…" he said.

"Twins," I said. "You know if you kill a pregnant woman, you can add a second murder count to the charges. You would have gotten three if you had finished the job. Does it feel worth it?"

He scowled. "You were trying to ruin my marriage."

"No, Raymond, you did that. Sarah came to me because she already suspected something. Now she just has proof. You stopped talking to her. Stopped coming home from work on time. She didn't need me to put two and two together – she came to me for proof. She already

91

knew. She just wanted something to bring to her lawyer. You did this. Not me."

The man banged his fists down on his table. "If I get out of here, I'll mow you down again. I should have gotten out of my truck and shot you in the head. You and that little pink haired errand boy punk."

"Wow," I said. "You made that way too easy. You're probably going to be in prison for a while now, Raymond." I crossed my arms. "Murder and attempted murder. It's not looking good for you."

Then he got still. "What are you talking about? I didn't kill anybody."

"Oh, didn't you, though?" I questioned. "Because Morgan isn't looking too good these days. You poisoned her with chloroform. Took her out to keep your secret just like you tried to take me out."

"Morgan?" he asked. His eyes become huge and he choked out, "What are you talking about?"

"Come on, Raymond," I said. "Don't try to play games. You already confessed to beating up a kid and assaulting me with a car. How did you manage to poison those brownies that killed your girlfriend?"

Raymond paled. "Killed my girlfriend? You mean Morgan's dead?" he asked, his voice raspy.

He was upset – like, really upset. Shaking and slobbery like, this was obviously news to him upset.

"I... I just talked to her a few days ago... told her I wanted to lay low for a while because I thought Sarah was getting suspicious. She's really dead?"

I could tell it wasn't an act. The man was horrified. I suppose even creepy Raymond cares about some people.

"Yeah," I said. "And, you better start talking."

"I didn't kill her!" Raymond yelped, his voice cracking. "What happened!"

"Someone poisoned her," I said. "Any idea who might want to hurt her?"

Raymond was too stunned to even think. He broke down crying and sniveling into his hands. He wasn't going to be any more use to me at this point, so I stood. When I exited the room, Deb was standing there along with three other officers and the stations local Chief.

"Nice," Deb said and gave me a thumbs-up.

"Excellent call letting her go in, Deb," the Chief said, and he took a moment to thank me for my assistance. I thanked them for helping me with my case as well. It was starting to look like I was managing to pull off just what Galigani had wanted me to do. Make some cop friends.

Deb walked me to a cubicle in the center of the station, and she sat down and pulled up a chair for me. She wanted to ask a few questions about the case I'd been working for Sarah since that was what had gotten Raymond all up in arms – just making sure she had everything covered when this went to court. And, of course, I told her I definitely wanted to press charges.

While I was sitting there, I took notice of Deb's desk. There was a picture frame on the corner of the desk, but it was turned down like she didn't want to look at it. There was a bunch of chocolate wrappers in her little trash bin, and tissues with what looked like mascara wiped away on it. I frowned when she looked up from her notebook.

"Are you doing okay?" I asked her, and she gave me this quizzical look. My eyes shifted toward the picture frame, and she sighed.

"Nice observation," she said and picked it up, looking at the picture. "Haven't finished cleaning off my desk since the breakup. A lot of mementos."

"I'm sorry to hear that," I said. "A rough breakup?"

"Yeah," she said. "It always is when someone cheats."

"Oh, wow," I said, frowning. "Men, right? That seems to be a theme right now."

"Women too," she said, and she sat the frame down in front of me where I saw a cheesy Christmas photo – Deb and another woman wearing matching Christmas sweaters, their faces squished into the frame of the photo with the other woman holding a mistletoe and squishing her lips against Deb's flushed cheeks.

"Oh!" I said. "I guess I shouldn't assume. I'm sorry. Was the breakup recent?"

"Three days ago," she said.

"How long had you two been together?" I asked.

"Five years," she said, and I felt my stomach twist for her when she said it.

I shook my head. "That's rough."

"Yes, it is," she said. "I think I need to unwind. I've been kind of pushing myself into work, and frankly that's not healthy."

I smiled. "You know, if you need to unwind, I'm doing a girl's night out tonight."

Deb seemed somewhat intrigued. "You don't know me."

"No," I said. "But, it never hurts to make a new friend."

"Didn't I hear you say you were pregnant?" she asked.

"It's going to be a wild, sober girl's night," I said, smirking.

She laughed. "You know what? I'm game. I think I could use a girl's night."

CHAPTER 12

$\mathcal{I}$ really needed a girl's night out, so I was pretty excited that Paula had decided to drag me out that night. Jim was staying at home with Laurie, getting some much-needed daddy-daughter time. He'd been working late at the office a good bit over the past several days, so he hadn't seen her much.

I met Mom and Paula at one of those nice Mexican chain restaurants – a place where Mom and Paula could get themselves some margaritas and where I could tackle my latest pregnancy craving – nachos.

We sat down in a booth, and Mom whipped open the menu. She always had the hardest time picking what she wanted to eat at Mexican restaurants because everything always sounded good to her. Mexican food was kind of her vice.

"I hope you two don't mind, but I invited a new friend tonight," I said. "She just texted me and said she's five minutes out."

"A new friend?" Paula questioned. "How dare you – you're not allowed to have other friends."

I laughed, and so did my Mom. "Who is your new friend?" Mom asked.

"Her name's Deb. I met her at the police station," I said.

"I hope she wasn't under arrest," Paula joked.

"She's the officer who arrested Raymond after the hit and run," I said. "And, she took a chance on me and let me work Raymond to get a confession on tape. It was pretty easy, honestly. He was ready to talk as soon as he saw me. He threatened me too, so they have that on recording. He's going to be going away for a very long time."

"Good," Mom said.

Deb arrived, and she looked positively stunning in her silky black, long sleeved V-neck. She plopped down in the booth next to Paula and stuck her hand out. "Deb Fisher," she said to Paula.

Mom introduced herself while sipping on her margarita. Deb nodded at the drinks. "And, here I thought partying with a pregnant woman meant I wasn't going to get to have a drink!"

"Please, we never let Kate stop us from having a little fun," my mom teased.

"Plus, she's going to make us do karaoke by the time this night is through," Paula said, pointing a finger in my mom's direction in an accusing manner. "And, if I'm going to have to suffer through that, you better believe I'm going to need to down this thing."

Deb nodded, her hair falling down on her shoulders in thick curls. "Good to know. Karaoke, huh? This sounds like my kind of group."

"Awesome, so you're down for karaoke?" I asked.

"Absolutely," she said. "They do that here?"

"Every Thursday night," Paula said.

Deb ordered herself a margarita when the server made her way over. We all ordered dinner, and with that our girls night officially kicked off. We laughed, got to know Deb, and just generally enjoyed ourselves. Halfway through our dinner, karaoke got going, and Mom and Deb scurried up on stage to do a duet together while Paula and I laughed and poked fun at them from the table. The moment allowed a little bit of alone time between Paula and me.

"So, how is the case coming?" Paula asked, and I shrugged.

"Could be better," I said. "A lot of cheaters, and I really don't like dealing with that. But, like Galigani said, in the PI business that's one of the most common cases I'm going to get stuck with. So, I guess I got to get used to it."

"Probably makes Jim seem like a saint, am I right?" Paula said, and she noticed me cringe. "Something going on with you and Jim?"

"I don't know... maybe. A part of me thinks it's just me being paranoid."

"What's going on?" she asked.

"I guess I'm just a little worried," I said. "It's probably this case that's doing it to me."

"How so?"

"Just dealing with Raymond, mostly," I said.

"Wait, don't you dare tell me you're worried that Jim might cheat on you," Paula jeered. "Kate, you have yourself a great man there. Don't get in your head."

"I know, I know," I said. "But, Jim... well, he lied to me, Paula. You know that café he has been going to for me to get those brownies?"

"Yeah?"

"His ex-girlfriend, from high school, she owns it. He had been going up there and seeing her, and he didn't tell me. Then, they got into some argument, and she called the cops on him. And, I found... text messages. She had texted him some weird smiley faces, and she messaged him and called him sexy!"

"Oh, come on, Kate... it's Jim. Are you sure you're not just reading things wrong?" Paula asked.

"I don't know, and that's the problem," I said. "Jim won't tell me anything. He doesn't want to talk about this Cassandra person. He's being so weird. It's making me antsy. And, let's be honest, I don't exactly look like I did when we first got married. I gained some weight with Laurie—"

"Come on, Kate. You've got to be kidding me. You look fantastic."

I shrugged. "I don't know. And now I'm pregnant again. I mean, it's twins!? I don't even want to think about what they're going to do to my figure. Maybe Jim isn't... attracted to me anymore?"

"That's ridiculous," Paula said. "Kate, listen to Paula. Jim adores you. He is a wonderful, wonderful husband. He treats you good.

You're just getting a taste of what it's like being married to an imperfect human being. Maybe he flirted a little bit with his ex-girlfriend because of just that – it's his ex-girlfriend. If they were texting, it was probably about your brownies and she was just being a little flirty because, well, they used to date. And, you know what? He might have even flirted back a little because it's someone he knows and is familiar with, and it was all just him being friendly because that's just Jim. He's called me *gorgeous lady* before – in front of you. He's a friendly guy. But, he's faithful. I don't doubt that."

I smiled. "Thanks, Paula. You're right. I'm just being... too..."

"Pregnant," we said together and laughed.

Mom and Deb plopped down at the table, and we congratulated them on the tipsy cat-screams they called singing. I was finally starting to feel better and relaxing into the evening when suddenly, Deb ducked behind her drink menu and started grumbling under her breath.

"You okay there, Deb?" Paula asked.

"I just saw my ex," she griped.

"Ooh, no," Paula said. "Need us to chase him off?"

Deb frowned. "Crud, she sees me."

We turned, and I saw the woman from the photo on Deb's desk. She was with another woman, walking arm in arm as she strutted her way over. "Deb!" she exclaimed. "Good to see you."

"Yeah, you too," Deb said uncomfortably.

"Who are your friends?" she asked.

Deb did a quick introduction, calling the woman Jasmine. Jasmine's partner just stood back, smiling with this very smug look on her face. Eventually the woman left, and she and the new girl found seats a good distance from us – thankfully.

"So, Jasmine is the ex?" Mom asked.

"Yes," Deb groaned.

"Is the woman she's with the woman she, um..." I paused, realizing I probably shouldn't be revealing too much information in front of Mom and Paula. She likely didn't want to talk about it.

"No, that wasn't her," Deb said. "I don't think Jasmine is quite trashy enough to come walking up to me with the woman she cheated on me with."

If only.

No, Jasmine had something just as trashy in mind. Ten minutes later, Jasmine and her new fling were up on stage singing *Constant Craving*. I saw Deb tense up, and I know Mom and Paula noticed it to.

"Something wrong?" my mom asked.

"It's nothing," Deb griped. "Well, not really. That was our song."

Jasmine kept glancing over – that same satirical smirk on her face.

"Ooh, I could break that little girl's nose," Mom said. "And, I could do it."

"Easy there, Mom," I said.

"I think I'm going to just go," Deb said.

"Then we're going with," Paula said and waved a server down. Paula threw everything on her card so that we could get out of there as quickly as possible. "We're going to go get some freaking ice cream," Paula declared, and Deb smiled at her.

"That sounds just perfect," Deb said as the server dropped off the check.

We all scooted out of the booths. Being a fatty pregnant lady, I shoveled a few more bites of what was left of my nachos into my mouth before scooting out of the booth. They all had a good laugh at that.

Of course, Jasmine couldn't resist sashaying over. "Leaving so soon?" she asked.

"Save it," I hissed, and I surprised myself at how sassy I sounded.

Jasmine even took a step back. "What's your problem?" she asked me.

"Walk away," I said, and she did. I'd sounded like an evil sorceress with the way the simple command had slipped from my lips, and I'm sure the scowl on my face also had done the job of striking some terror in her.

We headed out, and Deb started laughing once we made it to the parking lot. "I think you scared her," she said. "Thanks."

"Kate can be scary when she wants to be," Paula said. "You should see what she does to people who try to separate her from her nachos."

I pinched Paula's arm so hard, she shrieked.

"See what I mean?" she complained.

We crossed the street where there was a nice, family owned ice cream parlor that made some of the best homemade ice cream I've ever had in my life.

Maybe I'm still craving sweets.

Deb ordered herself a double scoop of double chocolate chunk ice cream, and it looked so good that I got myself the exact same thing and had them add some chocolate and caramel fudge. We sat around half the night in that ice cream parlor laughing and poking fun at Jasmine's awful rendition of *Constant Craving*.

Frankly, I'd had a wonderful time. And, I'd managed to make a cop buddy just as Galigani had instructed, and it'd been easier than I thought.

I was glad to have befriended Deb.

Just as we were finishing slurping up the last of the chocolate sauce, Deb said. "I got a warrant to search Raymond's house tomorrow."

My jaw dropped. "Can I go with you?" I blurted.

She laughed. "Of course not! I can't take you with me. That would be breaking every rule in the book."

I frowned. "Right, of course."

Deb shrugged. "But you know, if you just showed up there…"

I quirked an eyebrow at her. "What time would I just show up?"

"8 am," she replied.

Mom clapped her hands. "Kate! I want to see my grandbaby! Why don't I come by tomorrow around 8 am?"

I winked at her. "Thanks mom, you're the best."

I said farewell to Deb, Mom, and Paula after we returned to our vehicles. I drove home, a little later than I'd planned. Jim was already asleep, and he had managed to get Laurie down for bed as well. I wanted popcorn all of a sudden – as if I hadn't already eaten enough junk food that night. These kids were going to have very serious snacking problems.

I popped the popcorn and started chowing down, and boy was it amazing. But, then, sitting in my living room I suddenly got this weird feeling in the pit of my stomach.

Like, someone was watching me.

I looked up, glancing out my front window. I could almost swear that I saw a pair of eyes staring back at me. I jumped up and ran, flipping on my porch lights. No one was out there, but I definitely saw some taillights speeding off. Someone had been watching me through the window.

I double checked all the locks in the house and added *Get an Alarm System.* system to my to-do list. I thought about calling the police, but I was worried I'd come off as some crazy, paranoid woman.

Raymond was in jail, after all.

Who else could possibly be after me?

CHAPTER 13

I met Deb outside of Raymond and Sarah's home the next morning. Sarah had left the door unlocked for us – more than willing to let us look through the house if her soon-to-be ex-husband had been up to something sneaky. Sarah was across town taking care of some sort of business she couldn't get away from. Deb, along with about three other officers, arrived shortly after me.

One of the other officers squinted at me and growled at Deb. She said something in hushed tones that I couldn't overhear, but the man made a face at me and said nothing more.

We all spread out, searching the house for anything that could further convict Raymond. We already had him confess to attempting to kill me and beating up a teenager, but he had yet to confess to murdering Morgan. He was outright denying it, and frankly, he was our primary suspect at the time.

"What about Sarah?" Deb asked while I was snooping through some drawers in the couple's living room.

"What about her?" I asked.

"Could she have killed Morgan?" she asked.

"I mean, it's possible," I said. "But, from what I could tell when I showed her the pictures of Raymond and Morgan, she was pretty shocked by it all. She also acted like she had no idea who Morgan was. And, I believed her. It seemed like legitimate surprise. And, I didn't show her the pictures until after Morgan had been killed, so it's not like I tipped her off and then she went and killed her. Plus, Sarah seems kind of like a fragile individual. I don't think she has it in her to kill someone."

Deb grunted. "You'd be surprised."

We spent hours in that house, and frankly we didn't find anything condemning. One of the officers took Raymond's computer back to the station to sift through emails and browser history.

We checked every inch of that house, but didn't find anything that would convict him of murder.

"No smoking bottle of chloroform," I whined.

Deb laughed. "Well, I didn't expect that. He probably dumped the empty bottle. But I was hoping for at least a copy of the key to the bakery."

"You still think it was Raymond?" I asked.

"I do," Deb said. "He was willing to kill you to keep his secret. And, he beat up a kid. It sounds like he really wanted this secret to be kept. He was a creep, but he didn't want to ruin his marriage either. He was desperate and very violent. He could have resorted to murder. Maybe the techs will uncover something in his web browser search. Plus we have his credit card records subpoenaed. If he bought anything online or otherwise, we'll be able to track it.

"But, it's just like you said, Raymond is violent. He assaulted Kenny – bruising up the kids face. And, he rammed me with a car. If he wanted Morgan dead, poisoning doesn't really fit his style. Plus, our killer poisoned a plate of brownies. Cassandra was almost killed... maybe she was the intended target. Or, it could have been anyone at that party. Maybe Morgan was just collateral damage, and we're looking at this thing from the wrong angle?"

"If our killer hadn't been after Morgan, then we're at a loss," Deb said. "We have a list of everyone who was at the party, and it's extensive. There's the bakery workers, the actors, the stage crew, the playwright, and several friends and family members of anyone related to the show. We have no way of knowing who the intended target had been if it wasn't Morgan."

"The only thing we can do, it seems, is narrow it down," I said. "Maybe instead of trying to convict Raymond, we should be trying to prove his innocence?" Saying that literally made me throw up a little in my mouth.

"Prove his innocence?" Deb questioned. "That creep tried to kill you."

"Yeah, and I'm going to be very satisfied to see him go to jail for that, but even though I can't stand him doesn't mean I want to convict him of something he didn't do. If we can't prove he's guilty, maybe we should see if we could clear him of the crime instead of wasting our time on him. Like you said, there were a lot of people at that party. Raymond wasn't there. And, he punched a teenager in the face and ran into my car; poisoning brownies just doesn't seem like his MO."

"But he could have poisoned the brownies at the bakery, and dating Morgan, he probably had access to it," Deb argued.

"But, wouldn't it make sense for the killer to have been at the party? To try and make sure his intended victim ate the brownies?"

"Yes, unless our killer didn't care about collateral damage," Deb said. "But, you're right. Raymond gave us an alibi, said he was fishing with some buddies, but I haven't been able to track them down. Maybe I need to try a little harder and verify his story."

"While you're working on that, I'm going to call Sarah again. Go speak with her and see if she can give us any insight on Raymond. And, I'll go by the bakery to talk to the employees there as well. Maybe jog some of their memories and see if they remember seeing anything that day leading up to the party," I said, and Deb nodded.

"If the bakery workers give you a hard time, let me know, and I'll see what I can do about getting a warrant," Deb said.

"Sounds like a plan," I said, and we shook hands.

I kind of liked having a cop buddy. It sure was going to make things easier to work with the police instead of against them.

I called Sarah from the car where we decided on a place to meet. I pulled out of the neighborhood, and a few miles down the road I spotted the billboard. I laughed – hard. There was Raymond and Morgan, locking lips with her shoulder sensually exposed.

I'd taken that picture.

The tagline read, "My husband cheated: here's his information – feel free to let him know what you think!" followed by his phone number, email, place of business, and a few other ways to contact him through social media.

"Harsh," I said, but I was somewhat proud of the timid woman.

I pulled over on the side of the road. Sarah was standing there next to her car, admiring the giant billboard she'd rented. I inched my car forward and rolled down my window, smiling at her as she trotted up to me.

"What do you think?" she asked.

"Genius," I said.

"His parents saw it," she said. "I'm glad. They'll give him hell."

"Good," I said. "Listen, Sarah, we need to talk about Raymond and Morgan."

"You know... I'm really sorry about what happened to her," Sarah said. "I mean, I was angry when you told me that this woman was sleeping with my husband, but... well, I wouldn't wish that on anybody, you know? Not even Raymond. I mean, I did put this billboard up, so it's not like I'm a super forgiving person."

"I understand," I said. "Is Raymond usually a violent person?"

"No! That's the thing, he's not. I heard about what he did to you, and I'm so sorry. I don't understand. If he was so desperate to save our marriage, he should have just broken up with Morgan and come clean. Not this filthy sneaking around crap he's pulled. That's what I get for sending my husband to get cupcakes at Skank Bakery. I'm sure that's how they met – I sent him to get cupcakes I ordered for my mom for her birthday last year... I wonder if they've been together since then? Ugh, I don't even want to think about it."

I snorted slightly. "I'm sorry, Skank Bakery?" I questioned.

"That's the nickname a lot of people around here have for *Cassandra's Cookies*. All the women who work there are sort of notorious for dating married men," Sarah said.

"Oh, really?" I questioned.

"Yeah, it's just local gossip, but that's what I've heard," Sarah said. "I never imagined that Raymond would fall for that, though."

"I think I need to speak to some of the workers there," I said, gripping the steering wheel as I thought about Jim. "One more thing, did Raymond like to cook? Or bake? Or, you know, did he have any kitchen skills?"

Sarah barked a laugh. "Raymond? You've got to be kidding me? The only time he went near a kitchen was to fill his plate!"

The more Sarah and I chatted, the better I felt good about her. I didn't believe she or Raymond had anything to do with what happened to Morgan.

After I left, I called Deb. We cracked up on the phone with each other about the billboard, and I told her about my conversation with Sarah and that it had gone well.

"Yeah, I don't think she did it either," Deb said. "There's no evidence suggesting that. And, I just checked out Raymond's alibi. He and his buddies rented a fishing boat at Shasta. We have receipts and convenience store video tape footage. Alan is at the precinct downloading it now, but I think we'll find it's a pretty tight alibi."

"Dang," I said. "So, Raymond's not our guy, is he?"

"You were right, though," Deb said. "Now that we know he's not, we can refocus. You headed to the bakery?"

"I am," I said.

"Let me know how it goes. I'm getting a warrant, but they're being slow down here today. You're not a cop, and Cassandra seems to like you. Maybe you can sweet talk your way into looking around," Deb suggested.

I agreed. Cassandra would likely be back to work today and hopefully be agreeable to my inquiries.

As soon as I stepped inside the colorful bakery, I spotted her behind the counter. She still looked a little pale, but better.

"Hey, Kate!" she said. "Oh my goodness! What happened to you?"

I rubbed at my temple, that still had a small bandage on it. "Long story," I said. "Perils of being a PI."

She made a pouty face for me. "I'm sorry. Can I get you one of your special brownies?"

"No thanks," I said. "I think that craving has finally been satisfied. It took eating so many that it made me physically sick to get over it, though. You're quite a baker."

"Thanks!" Cassandra said, smiling. "What can I help you with?"

"Would you mind if I spoke with some of your employees about Morgan?" I asked.

"Of course," she said. "I did hire you, remember? Feel free to talk and look around or whatever you need to do."

That was easy.

Maybe I really do have a knack for investigations?

"I will," I said.

I spoke with a few employees, and outright asked about Morgan's love life again. Once more, they confirmed she dated married men, and it sounded like quite a few of the girls there shared similar dating life. I wanted to punch them – all of them. But, I had to remain professional.

I strolled into the back, finding Cassandra's work office.

"Well, she did say I could look around," I said under my breath as I made my way past the *Employees Only* sign. Cassandra's desk was fairly plain, a few decorations from some sorority she'd been in during college. A framed diploma from a culinary academy. A picture of what was probably her dog sat by her computer. I went to pick up the picture, and I unintentionally jiggled her mouse. Her Facebook page was pulled open. I glanced over my shoulder – no one was coming, so I sat down.

I looked at the messenger app, and sure enough Jim's name popped up. My palms were sweating as I found myself debating on whether or not to check. I did, and I got an eye full of... naked Cassandra.

"Oh, you've got to be kidding me," I practically growled. She sent Jim naked pictures!

My ears and cheeks grew warm. If I was a cartoon, steam would have started spewing out of my ears and nostrils. I gripped the mouse, and wanted to slam it into her monitor.

I'll kill her!

No, I was going to do this right. I grabbed my thumb drive and copied over the screenshots. Then I immediately deleted my screenshots so she wouldn't know what I'd done. On impulse, I copied her entire delete folder on to my thumb drive, then emptied.

I stood, taking a moment to compose myself before leaving the office. As I was leaving, Cassandra spotted me from where she stood behind the counter.

"You leaving already?" she asked me curiously.

Yeah, so I don't punch you, I thought, but I just smiled and acted like nothing was wrong. "Yeah, got to get back home to my kiddo."

You home wrecker!

"I understand. Listen, if there's anything else I can do to help with the case, please let me know. Morgan was my friend, you know?"

She seemed sad. I wanted to strangle her, but I had a job to do. I needed to separate whatever was going on with her and Jim from the case – I needed to get justice for Morgan whether she was a cheat like Cassandra or not.

"I'll let you know," I said and hurried out, stopping by the store to grab some more printer ink before driving home.

Mom was at my house watching Laurie, and she asked me what felt like a million questions, but I feigned tiredness and promised to call her later after I napped. First order of business, I took care of Laurie, feeding her, bathing her, and then putting her down for a nap before heading into my and Jim's home office.

I started crying, but I kept working. I printed the pictures of Cassandra and placed them on the kitchen table. I scanned her deleted folder, but it seemed full of old security videos from the bakery camera. I ignored those and kept on working.

By the time I was done, I was shaking.

Then, I waited.

Whiskers seemed to realize how upset I was and settled into my lap.

I received a friendly, "On my way home, babe!" text from Jim, and as per usual I told him to drive safe.

At this point, I had way too much anger and sadness built up.

I mean, naked pictures! How could there possibly be an excuse for that? This woman was sending him nudes! I kept looking at the pictures laid out on my kitchen table, and every once in a while, I'd choked up.

It was just too much. I started thinking about Raymond and Sarah – Deb's relationship, Butterfly and Kenny. Heck, even Vicente's stupid play was about cheaters! They disgusted me. I saw no excuse for it.

None.

Yet, here I was, sitting in my kitchen, waiting to confront my husband about it.

Had Jim cheated on me? Even if he didn't, had he willingly accepted these pictures from Cassandra? And, didn't that count as cheating?

Jim came through the door and Whiskers jumped from my lap and arched her back.

"Laurie sleeping?" I heard him say as he rounded the corner into the kitchen. He glanced over to see what I was doing and saw the pictures, and his face went pale.

I practically hissed at him. "We I need to talk."

CHAPTER 14

*Y*eah, that escalated really quickly. Never call a pregnant woman crazy and paranoid – because as soon as those words slipped out of Jim's lips, I lost it. I started screaming and throwing my hands around like I'd truly lost my mind.

"Well, Jim, what do you expect me to think?" I questioned him, my fists shaking at my side.

"You're supposed to trust me – that's what!" he snapped back.

"Trust you? How can I trust you, when you won't even tell me what's going on!" I shouted, my whole body joining my fists in shaking. "First of all, you've been secretly going to see your ex-girlfriend—"

"I haven't secretly been seeing her! I was going there to get you your brownies!"

"You didn't tell me, Jim! That's the point! You didn't tell me that the bakery was owned by your ex!"

"You're right, I didn't," he said. "But, only because I didn't think it was worth mentioning. We dated briefly in high school. We hardly spoke at all the first few times I went into the bakery. I didn't even realize it was her at first."

"*Second*," I said, holding up two fingers. "Secondly, you didn't tell me you had the police called on you!"

"I didn't want you to freak out," he said.

"Well, I'm freaking out now, Jim!" I snarled. "And, I know you have her cell phone number in your phone!"

"Oh my God, Kate, have you seriously been going through my phone?" he asked.

"You've been texting her! And, she keeps sending you all these flirty emojis, and then I find this—" I pointed toward all the erotic photos spread out across our kitchen table.

"Where did you even find that?" he asked.

"She left her Facebook logged in when I went to the bakery to interview some of the employees," I said. "And, she had sent those to you!"

Jim sat down at the table; he started snatching up the photos and crumpling them up in his frustration. "You're unbelievable," he told me.

"Me!" I shrieked. "I'm unbelievable? Are – are you kidding me! Look at all this, Jim! Are you seriously questioning why I'm upset right now?" I took a breath, and that pause made me break down. I started crying. I lost all the confidence I had gathered prior to the confrontation and Jim looked up at me with these sad eyes. "Are you sleeping with her, Jim?" I asked.

"God, babe, no!" he said and jumped up. "Kate, I would never hurt you like that. Look... just... sit down. I'm going to make some coffee, and I'll explain what's going on, okay?"

This should be good, I thought and collapsed on a chair at the table, arms crossed. We didn't speak while the coffee was brewing. I was too upset to talk, and he was very timid – he kept shaking his head and muttering to himself. He set a cup of coffee in front of me – plenty of sugar just like I liked it, and he poured a tiny bit of creamer for me before sitting down and taking a swig of his coffee, cringing as he burnt his tongue.

I shook my head; he always burnt himself with coffee when he was distracted.

Idiot!

He took a breath. "Okay, so I haven't been totally open with you about what's going on. I'll admit that, and I'm sorry, Kate. I never meant to get you upset or make you worry. I love you, Kate. And, I would never do anything intentionally to hurt you. I hope you know that."

He reached for my hand, but I crossed my arms and gave him my stone face. I was willing to listen, but it better be good or I'd kill him.

"Right," he said to himself more than to me. "The first time I went to the bakery Cassandra wasn't there. I had no idea she owned it. Then, you just really liked them, remember?" I nodded, and he continued. "So, I kept going back. I'd see her, but I honestly didn't recognize her. It was high school, you know? And, we didn't even date that long. Just a little in junior year, I think. Anyway, one day we're talking, and she starts flirting with me. I turned her down, told her I was happily married. That's the God's honest truth, Kate. I thought she was a lunatic redhead. I mean, you know, what I'm trying to say. I'm not even interested in anyone else, because I'm in love with you. But if I was single, she… she… wouldn't interest me."

He stopped talking to look at me and see if things were moving in his favor.

I made a face to indicate to him that they weren't, then sipped my coffee.

He nodded, understanding he still had an uphill battle. "So she told me she was Cassandra from high school. And we both just laughed about it. She told me a little about college and culinary school, and I told her about you and Laurie and the new baby. Just catching up. I thought everything was normal. She talked me into exchanging numbers; she was being friendly and told me that if you were ever craving anything at weird hours to just hit her up, and she'd be happy to swing by early or stay late for me, since we were friends."

"So, that's why her number is in your phone?" I asked.

"Yes," he said. "And, at first, it was fine. We just texted about brownies, and I think I sent her a picture of Laurie once. That was it. But, then she just started texting me more. She friended me on Facebook, and I accepted – not thinking anything about it. She kept texting me about random stuff – innocent at first. She sent a picture of her dog. Then one day she sent me a picture of herself – it was fairly innocent – just her in a dress asking me what I thought. I ignored the text because I thought it was inappropriate, and the next time I went into her shop she asked me why I didn't respond. I told her I didn't think it was appropriate, and she acted like she understood. She even apologized. But, later that night I got a message from her on my phone, and she had sent me a picture of her cleavage and made some joke about whether or not it was inappropriate. I told her to stop."

"And, what, it just escalated?" I asked.

"Yes," Jim said. "I went into the shop the next day and told her to knock it off, and she grabbed me... um..." his face turned bright red. He cleared his throat. "She grabbed me *inappropriately*, and I pushed her back." Jim sat back, looking quite embarrassed. "She fell back into one of her workers, and they knocked a whole tray of cookies down. Cassandra called the police and said I assaulted her, and I told the police what happened, but they didn't really believe me. Cassandra chose not to press charges, and we moved on. She apologized, I apologized, and that was it. I didn't tell you about it because, well, I don't know why... I think I was hoping the whole thing would just go away."

I nodded toward the pile of crumpled up paper. "And, the pictures?" I asked.

"I blocked her on Facebook as soon as I saw those in my inbox," he said and handed me his phone. "Look for yourself."

I did. I wasn't playing around at this point. He also pulled open the conversation I had seen only a bit of when I had spied at the hospital. He had ignored her several times. He never responded whenever she sent him flirtatious emojis, and there was even a whole conversation from a week or two before with Jim telling her to stop flirting – that he was married and didn't find it cute.

I felt awful. I sunk down in my seat. "Why didn't you just tell me?" I asked.

"I thought you had enough to worry about," he said. "I just handled it, or at least, I thought I had. I ignored her advances, and I only ever went to the shop to get you those brownies. It was getting close to the point that I was going to tell you I couldn't keep going back there, though. But, I started ordering them ahead of time so all I had to do was go and pick them up. And, I'm sure you noticed, I started buying them in bulk instead of just picking up one or two for you so that I wouldn't have to go back as often."

Yeah, I had noticed that. I had just thought he was tired of always having to go out to get my brownies. "Jim, I'm sorry," I said.

"Kate, I'm sorry," he said and reached across the table to me to take my hand. "I should have just told you what was going on. I mean, it sure would have saved us both a lot of heartache. I just didn't want you to worry. I'm sorry I made you think that I would ever do something to hurt you. I love you. I would never cheat on you, Kate."

I smiled at him. "I love you too. I just wish you would have talked to me about all this. I think I've spent more time worrying about this than actually investigating the case your ex-girlfriend hired me for."

Jim shook his head. "Yeah, about that. I don't want this to come out wrong because you're an amazing detective and all, but I'm pretty sure she just hired you to bug me."

"I think you're probably right," I said and laughed. "It worked, though, didn't it?"

"It did," he said. "But, that probably could have been resolved if I had just talked to you." He shook his head and sat upright. "Gosh, Kate, I feel terrible. I feel so lucky to have you, you know? I wouldn't do anything to jeopardize that. You're beautiful, smart, sexy – and, you're an amazing mom. I don't want any woman but you. You know that, right?"

"I do," I said. "I guess a lot of this was just me being paranoid. I've felt really insecure, honestly. My body changed so much from Laurie, and I got pregnant again so quickly... I haven't even finished losing all the baby weight from Laurie! Now, twins? I guess I just don't feel like myself anymore."

"You're beautiful, babe," he said. "You're the mommy of them. I love you. I love the family we're building."

"Look at you being all sweet," I said, and he jumped up and hurried over to my side, pulling me up to my feet to give me a big hug and kiss. My toes curled a little. I rested my head on his chest, and he squeezed me tight. I had a good man there, and I knew it then.

I really wanted to give Cassandra a black eye for putting me in this situation. She made me doubt my husband, and I hated it. I hated that I didn't just trust him. But, I needed to let it go for the time being. Cassandra, albeit a bit of a tramp, was still my client, and I had promised to find out what had happened to Morgan.

"Hey, baby?" Jim spoke as we pulled apart.

"Yeah?" I asked, noticing his befuddled look.

"Um… where's Laurie?" he asked.

"Sleeping," I said.

"Oh, yeah?" he said, this sly little smile appearing on his face.

"Yeah?"

"Good," he said, and he scooped me right up. I squealed, laughing hysterically as he literally swooped me right off my feet. He whooshed me into the living room, and the two of us fell onto the couch in a fit of laughter and kisses. I think I needed that. I was overdue for some good attention from my husband, and I think he realized that.

Such an awful afternoon had turned into such a great evening at home with Jim.

We retired to bed. I was exhausted. Something about harboring so much anger and resentment all day only to have it pulled out from under you just leaves you feeling exhausted. Before drifting off to sleep, I grabbed my notepad and pen I keep on my nightstand. I had a lot of stuff to do the next day, so I started jotting down my to-do list. Jim didn't go to sleep right away; he laid on his side looking up at me with a flirty smile that caused me to blush. "What?" I asked.

"Just looking at you," he said. "We should do a date night. Soon. It's been a while."

"We went to that play," I said.

"Date night does not count if someone dies while you're out," he said. "It puts a damper on things. I mean, a real date night. Dinner and a movie. Somewhere nice."

I nodded. "That sounds like an incredible idea." I leaned over and kissed him, and he rolled over – falling asleep instantly. I'm still jealous of his ability to do that. I get too into my head at night – thinking about what all I need to do. The to-do list at the bedside helps keep me from thinking too much. By the time I was finished and ready for bed, I had a pretty extensive list ahead of me:

To Do:

1. Doctor's Appointment
2. Pick out new car seats for the twins
3. Larger stroller?
4. Check out the thrift store for baby clothes
5. Go through Laurie's old clothes too
6. Call Deb
7. Go see Paula today! – bring food?
8. Revisit the bakery
9. Solve a murder – try not to kill Cassandra in the process

CHAPTER 15

*T*he following morning, I headed off, Laurie in tow, to a doctor's appointment. With everything going on, the doctors were being extra cautious about my pregnancy. Not only was it a higher risk pregnancy due to the twins, but also because I'd suffered that carbon monoxide poisoning last month.

Thankfully this time, my blood work came back looking a little better – but they said that my oxygen level in my blood was still a tad low. Not like it had been, so it was improving. It seemed weird to me that the oxygen level in my blood was taking so long to get back to normal. The poisoning incident had been a month before.

Why was it taking so long for me to get better?

Laurie began to fuss in her carrier, so I scooped her out and sat her in my lap as we waited for Dr. Green to return. When she entered, she handed me some pamphlets about smoking and pregnancy.

I frowned. "What's this?"

"Well, we just like to make sure moms are informed on the dangers of smoking while pregnant," Dr. Green said.

"Oh, I don't smoke," I said, handing the pamphlets back to her.

"Are you on a nicotine patch?" she asked me.

"Um... no?" I questioned, very confused. "I've never smoked before."

Now Dr. Green looked confused. We were just two very confused ladies staring back at one another. "Are you sure about that, Kate?" Dr. Green asked. "There's no need to lie to me. I'm your doctor, and I'm here to help you in any way I can. I can prescribe something for you that could help, and there are other means of dealing with a smoking habit that can be safer for the babies other than a nicotine patch?"

"Dr. Green, I'm not on a nicotine patch. And, I've never smoked a day in my life," I said.

"Kate, there are traces of nicotine in your blood sample," Dr. Green said.

"Well, that can't be right," I said. "Something must be wrong. I promise I'm not lying. I've never smoked before."

Dr. Green didn't seem very convinced, but she ordered another blood test and wanted the hospital to do it. I sighed and added that to my to-do list. It was always a bummer when you scratch something off your to-do list and then immediately have to add something to it. One step forward, one step back. Not the way I liked to work.

Thankfully, I was able to head straight to the hospital. The nurse there was nice and quick, albeit not as gentle as the tech in Dr. Green's office. I'd have a bruise on my arm, I was sure.

She told me they'd send the sample to the lab and then the results to Dr. Green.

Okay, so my to-do list was looking a little better now:

To Do:

1. ~~Doctor's Appointment~~
2. Pick out new car seats for the twins
3. Larger stroller?
4. Check out the thrift store for baby clothes
5. Go through Laurie's old clothes too
6. Call Deb

7. Go see Paula today! – bring food?
8. Revisit the bakery
9. Solve a murder – try not to kill Cassandra in the process
10. ~~Go get blood test~~

THERE WERE a lot of fun items on my list – baby shopping was a personal favorite. There was an adorable boutique near the hospital, that was hard to resist. Unfortunately, I didn't know if I was shopping for boys or girls or both just yet, so I resisted getting any clothing. However, the boutique did sell some other necessary baby items.

We needed a large stroller that carried two, possibly three babies. I was trying to decide whether or not a three baby stroller for Laurie and her younger siblings would be worth the buy or if just a stroller for twins would be enough. A three baby stroller would be huge, I figured, but sure enough my favorite baby boutique came through for me.

They had this sweet umbrella-like stroller that was for three kiddos. It had baby blue décor over the mostly silver stroller, so I felt like it wasn't too gender-specific. Unfortunately, they only had the one on the floor left, and it was damaged, so they had to order one for me.

I didn't care. I was very excited to have one ordered, and they promised delivery in three weeks – plenty of time before baby number two and three got there. And, I found some affordable car seats that weren't too big and bulky, so I went ahead and got those as well. I loved this place. It was huge, but it was also quaint and adorable.

One of the girls who was working kindly helped me put the boxed car seats into the back of my vehicle, and soon Laurie and I were off. I swung by the thrift store on the way home, and snagged anything that seemed even remotely gender neutral, lots of yellows and greens. We'd have ducks and frogs coming out of our ears.

A feeling of accomplishment soothed me as I drove home. Once there, I fed Laurie, and set her up to play in the living room while I brought everything in from the car. Then I put Laurie down for a nap, and I suddenly had this burst of energy.

Something about knocking out half your to-do list fairly quickly really gave you the motivation to keep going.

Why can't every day be this?

Just as I was struggling to getting Laurie down for a nap, my phone buzzed with a text from Paula.

"Free to meet me downtown?"

We texted back and forth and she sent me an address with a request to bring lunch.

Laurie was going through a phase where she loved napping in the car, so I decided a ride downtown would be ideal for us both.

I swung through a drive-through, then headed downtown. I munched on salty fries as Laurie snoozed peacefully in her car seat.

The address Paula had sent me was for a large apartment complex across town, that she had been bugging me about coming to see. When I arrived, Laurie and to-go bags in tow, I was blown away by the elegance of the place. The apartment complex was one of the nicest places Paula had managed to book.

She had only had a few clients since getting back to work after having Chloe, and this one, so far, was the crown jewel of her projects. She met me out front and snagged Laurie from me, giving her a few snuggles until Laurie started to giggle.

"My little fellas are with my sister," Paula said. "She's been really great about supporting me with this new business venture."

"I'm glad to hear that," I said, and the two of us entered the lovely apartment building. The lobby looked amazing thanks to Paula's incredible decorating skills. She had some plants and gorgeous golden pots set up – the hints of greenery really added to the inviting feel of the lobby.

We sat down and ate, and she thanked me profusely for the food, since she was still breastfeeding three-month old Chloe, I knew she was as ravenous as I was. Then we headed upstairs and she showed off all the completely refurbished rooms she staged. I was so proud of her.

"How did you book this?" I asked.

"Believe it or not, the apartment building's owner came to your mom's play," Paula said. "She called me and told me she loved the set and that the play had been hilarious."

I cringed. "I still feel kind of bad for Domingo," I admitted. "He and I have had our spats, but he had put a lot of work into that play to have someone twist it into a cheesy comedy musical. I don't know. I can't imagine he's too happy about that."

"I know what you mean, but doesn't he take himself altogether too seriously?"

I chuckled. "That he does."

Paula shrugged. "But, I'm sure glad to have gotten a job like this out of it."

After sitting down in one of the rooms that was done up with a beautiful silver and teal color theme, I pulled out my to-do list. "You and your lists," Paula teased.

I glared at her. "I know you have very detailed to-do lists as well," I said. "How else could you possibly stay sane?"

"You're right," Paula said, smirking. I smiled as I went through my list, scratching things off:

To Do:

1. ~~Doctor's Appointment~~
2. ~~Pick out new car seats for the twins~~
3. ~~Larger stroller?~~
4. ~~Check out the thrift store for baby clothes~~
5. ~~Go through Laurie's old clothes too~~
6. Call Deb
7. ~~Go see Paula today! – bring food?~~
8. Revisit the bakery

9. Solve a murder – try not to kill Cassandra in the process
10. ~~Go get blood test~~

"WELL, LOOK AT YOU!" Paula said, glancing over my shoulder. "You've had a busy day."

"Yeah," I said. "It's been working out pretty well. I had a good groove at the start of the day. I've got more energy today than I've had lately. This case is driving me crazy, though. I think I'm looking at it from the wrong angle. I assumed that Morgan had been the intended target, but what if it had been Cassandra? I think I need to talk to her again, but she is the last person I want to talk to. Did I tell you what she did?"

"What?" Paula asked curiously.

"She has been flirting with Jim. Jim turned her down, of course, but it was a lot more serious than I originally thought. She sent him nudes, and he deleted her off his Facebook," I said, and Paula's eyes widened.

"Oh, wow! You need me to take her out for you?" she asked.

"No, I'm good. No more bodies, please," I said, taking a breath. "Jim and I talked about it, and I feel a little better now. I'm mad and upset, but she's not really worth it. And, besides, I need to prove to myself that I can be professional. She is a client, after all."

"What if whoever killed Morgan was going after one of the guests?" Paula suggested.

"That would probably make Domingo a suspect," I said. "His play had been ruined, but what are the chances that only the employees managed to get poisoned? I don't know. There is something I'm not seeing." I checked my phone for the time. "It's almost three. Maybe I should call Deb and see if she has anything for me."

"There's never enough time in the day," Paula said.

"No, there's not," I said, waving my to-do list around. "I don't think I'm going to solve a murder today." I took out my phone and gave Deb a call, and oh my goodness. She was drunk.

"Hey, Katie- pie!" she called into the phone.

"Deb?" I questioned.

"Hey, that's my name!" she yelped.

"Are you drunk?" I questioned.

"Shh… it's a secret," she said.

"Oh, you've got to be kidding me, where are you?" I questioned. Deb was supposed to have been working on getting me a lead, but apparently, she was getting wasted at three o'clock in the afternoon. Way too early to already be so drunk that she would start singing into the phone.

How do I manage to befriend a drunk cop?

Deb gave me the name of the bar, and I demanded she wait for me because I was going to collect her. She started ranting about her ex, but I hung up on her.

Paula offered to watch Laurie for me, but I told her not to worry about it.

How difficult would it be to go pick up Deb? She sounded drunk but not like an angry drunk.

I said farewell to Paula, and I drove down the road to this bar I'd never heard of.

It was called *Lady Luck*, and I soon found out why I never heard of it. It was a lesbian bar. I entered, baby on my hip, in search for my drunk cop friend. Deb was talking with some woman who was covered in head-to-toe tattoos.

I cleared my throat, causing the woman to spin around. "Sorry, I'm here to pick up that one there," I said, nodding toward Deb.

"Dang, girl, you're in trouble," the woman said as she looked at me and gave Deb a gentle nudge in my direction.

"Kate!" Deb yelped excitedly. "I just threw up in the bathroom!"

"Good for you, Deb," I said. "Come on, are you paid up?"

"She's paid up," the woman who had been lingering around her said. "Sorry, didn't know she was with someone."

"Uh… yeah," I said, grabbing Deb under her arm. I'm sure this looked like a lesbian wife coming to the bar to pick up the other mother of her child.

But who cared. I needed Deb and I needed her sober.

A few women snickered as I dragged Deb out of there and forced her into the passenger seat of my car. I hooked Laurie in and pulled out of the parking lot.

"Wow, I can't believe you're drunk. It's not even three thirty!" I snapped.

"It's five o'clock somewhere," Deb sang happily.

"Are you an alcoholic?" I asked.

She smiled at me. "Only on Tuesdays."

I rolled my eyes. "Today is Wednesday."

"It is?" Deb asked surprised. "No wonder the drinks were full price. They normally do a Two on Tuesday special."

I reached into the backseat pocket, where I had snacks stashed and pulled out a water bottle for her. "Here," I said.

Deb drank the water greedily then wiped her mouth with the back of her hand. "Wednesday?" She asked again, thoughtful. "Oh shoot. I have to work the night shift tonight!" Deb said, sitting upright with wide eyes. "Oh, jeez, I forgot I have to work tonight!"

"You're drunk!" I yelped.

"Oh, I'm so fired!" she hiccupped, rubbing her temples. "I'm so drunk! Ooh, I want something chocolate…"

"You're kidding," I said, shaking my head. I finally become buddies with a cop – get my inside woman – and she's probably going to get herself fired. "Okay, relax, when do you go into work?"

"Um… eight…" she said.

"Okay, plenty of time to sober you up," I said. "I need to go speak with Cassandra about my case anyway. Since you want chocolate, we'll get you something sweet to put some food on your stomach, and I'll have her make you a cup of strong coffee too. They have a barista station there."

"I love you, Katie," Deb told me, laying her head back. I reached over and smacked her awake.

I wasn't about to let her get fired. I needed this drunk goofball, and frankly I was beginning to think of her as a friend. I got her talking, and turns out she had done something very stupid earlier today. She'd called her ex and had left a very embarrassing message. Something clingy and desperate, and then she'd felt like an idiot and had decided to go drink her sorrows away.

I vowed on the drive over to *Cassandra's Cookies* that I wouldn't mention what I knew about her and Jim; it would only further complicate the case.

When we finally got to the shop, I sat Deb down by the window and told her to stay put. She waited while I ordered her a black coffee and a plate of chocolate cookies. I ordered myself a cup of coffee as well.

Cassandra sashayed over, putting the plate of cookies down in front of us as well as the two cups of coffee. "We'll be here for at least another hour doing closing duties," Cassandra said, nodding toward the two other employees who were still in the shop. The closed sign was already up. "Feel free to hang out at least that long, and we can chat more about Morgan's case too."

"I appreciate it, Cassandra," I said, trying not to grit my teeth in her direction. Cassandra trotted off to go help her employees with closing duties while I forced Deb to drink her coffee.

"Thanks for helping me," Deb muttered under her breath as she sipped on the coffee.

"Anytime," I said, pulling out my phone. I called Jim, explaining to him that I was taking care of a friend who had gotten a little tipsy and that I had found myself at Cassandra's shop.

"Why are you there?" he groaned.

"It's for the case, babe," I said. "But, I know you probably don't want to come by here, but can you come pick up Laurie on your way home, so I can get Deb taken care of?"

"Of course," Jim groaned into the phone. "I'm fifteen minutes out."

"Sounds good," I said, hanging up the phone. "Okay, Deb, finish up your coffee. You feeling any better?"

"I only see one of you now," she groaned, rubbing her temples and shaking her head.

"Okay, next I'm going to make you drink some more coffee. After

Jim gets here, I'll take you home, and you can take a cold shower before you go into work," I said.

"You're a life saver," Deb said, finishing off her cup of coffee.

I headed to the counter, ordering a final cup for Deb before they dumped out the coffee for the day.

CHAPTER 16

*D*eb was just sobering up enough to where I didn't feel like she was a danger to herself, so I set Laurie up in a high chair at the table with her while I ordered. The girl working behind the counter, a twenty-something woman named Trixie, told me the little muffin was on the house since they were going to be throwing them out that night anyway.

They were still soft, so I wasn't too worried about letting Laurie nibble on some bits and pieces. By that point, Cassandra had wandered off somewhere around the shop – I think she was signing for a delivery.

Trixie hadn't been at the bakery the last time I had come by to interview employees. So she and I chatted a bit.

I watched Deb from a safe distance as she crumbled up bits of muffin for Laurie. The woman was looking better as well as looking very thankful for my coming to her rescue.

I turned back to Trixie, bringing up Morgan. "Did you know her well?" I asked.

"Yeah," Trixie said sadly. "We're all pretty close here. I can't imagine someone wanting to hurt Morgan or Cassandra... well..."

"Well?" I questioned, trying to pull something out of her that I could use.

"I mean, a lot of the women around here, Morgan and Cassandra included, have a thing for married men," Trixie said. "Eventually someone was going to get really ticked, you know?"

"Yeah, but I cleared Morgan's sugar daddy and his wife," I said. "Were there any other men apart from Raymond she was seeing?"

"Not recently," Trixie said.

"What about Cassandra?" I asked, and Trixie got a little timid.

"I'm going to level with you," I said. "I know all about Cassandra attempting to seduce my husband."

"Oh... so you knew about that," Trixie said, looking embarrassed. "You know, Cassandra is actually a really awesome person. I don't approve of that... lifestyle, but she's not..."

"You don't need to explain anything to me," I said. "I'm a professional. I'm here to work. If there is anything more you could tell me, I'd appreciate it."

"I guess maybe you could talk to Cassandra about other guys she or Morgan have been dating," Trixie said. "But, I don't know who would have had access to the back of the bakery. Cassandra keeps this place locked up pretty good."

"I understand," I said, and then from the corner of my eye I spotted a camera. "You have security cameras?" I questioned.

"Yeah," Trixie said. "The police already skimmed through them, though, looking to see if anyone came into the back of the bakery the day those orange brownies were poisoned. But, no one other than the employees were back there, and they didn't see anything suspicious. In fact, the only ones the police say they saw on the video near the poisoned brownies were Cassandra and Morgan."

I nodded, thinking to myself for a moment. "Would you mind if I had a second glance? Maybe I can see something they missed?"

"Sure," Trixie said. "The footage I think is still pulled out and sitting on Cassandra's desk from when she let the police look at it."

I turned toward Deb. It was a small bakery, so I felt okay leaving her gradually more sober self there with Laurie for a bit.

"You good?" I asked her. "If I go look in the back for a second."

"I'm good enough to watch your kiddo while she nibbles on a muffin, yes," Deb said, shaking her head. "If she starts crying, though, I'm bringing her straight to you."

"Jim should be here any minute," I said. "I'll just be in the back for a second." Deb nodded, and I headed to the back where Cassandra's office was. I shivered a bit. Last time I had been in that office, I had found those ridiculous pictures she had sent Jim. I started feeling myself getting angry again, but I reminded myself that Jim had handled it well. He had told her to back off, confronted her about it, and had deleted her off his social media pages. She had gotten turned down; I didn't have anything to worry about.

I started watching the video from Cassandra's computer, and I specifically watched the video from the camera that was in the bakery's kitchen. Sure enough, just as Trixie had said, the only ones in the back of the bakery that evening before the play were Morgan and Cassandra.

I watched as they frosted the brownies.

That didn't make much sense.

When had they put the brownies in the oven? There seemed to be something missing from tape.

I froze.

Remembering Cassandra's delete folder I clicked on it, only to find that it was empty. But wait! I'd copied it onto my thumb drive. I ran back to the lobby and startled Deb.

"What's up?" she asked.

"Nothing," I whispered. "Give me a minute I need to check something out." I dug into the pockets of Laurie's stroller and located my key ring with the drive. "Don't let anyone go back there, okay?"

Deb gave me a half salute, which wasn't too confidence inspiring, but I decided to take my chances.

I rushed back to the office and stuffed the drive into the USB port. I located the video tape based on the time files and hit play.

Cassandra and her red hair filled the screen. She was mixing two different batches of brownies simultaneously.

Well, okay, maybe that was just due to volume… but …

Then, I saw something odd. Morgan stepped out of the bakery for a minute, and Cassandra pulled something out of a cabinet down below. My eyes widened as she poured some sort of liquid into one of the brownie batters.

There's no way, I thought to myself.

Cassandra wouldn't have poisoned herself, right?

Surely, if she had been trying to kill Morgan for whatever reason, she wouldn't have eaten the poisoned brownies herself.

I watched as she placed both batches of brownies into the oven and left the bakery. I continued watching the feed as Cassandra returned, and she and Morgan worked on a few more dishes for the party. Cassandra pulled the brownies out of the oven, poisoned batch and non-poisoned batch, and sat them on the counter.

Another staff member opened the door and peeked in, and called Cassandra to the front of the bakery.

Then I watched as Morgan picked up one of the pans and moved it to the other side of the first one so that she could make room for another baking project. The brownies got switched! Morgan, of course, must not have known that Cassandra was planning on poisoning someone, right?

I kept watching as Cassandra returned and proceeded to decorate the first pan, the pan she believed to be the poisoned brownies, with purple icing.

Purple icing?

Chills ran up my spine and my mouth went dry.

Oh my Lord.

She wanted Jim. She wanted *my* husband. The person she was trying to eliminate was *me.*

I watched in stunned silence as Cassandra then decorated the other batch, the one that was actually the poisoned batch, with orange icing.

She didn't know Morgan had switched the pans!

The two women has some sort of conversation, and Cassandra cut into the orange icing brownies, and the two women dug in – satisfying a sweet tooth craving, Morgan more so than Cassandra.

They laughed and chatted like two co-workers for a moment before packing up the brownies and the other items.

I couldn't believe this lunatic, this hussy, home wrecker had been planning to murder me!

And poor Morgan had been an innocent victim.

I grabbed the thumb drive and jammed it into my pocket. Rage pulsed out of me as if I were a cartoon. I headed straight for the kitchen. Trixie wasn't back there, so I assumed she was doing closing duties on the floor. I opened up the bottom cabinet, where I'd seen Cassandra pull out the bottle, but found it empty.

Darn!

No smoking bottle of Chloroform.

Well, I guess, she's not that stupid. She got rid of the evidence.

I rummaged around the cabinet and behind a box of sugar, I saw some strange brownish residue. I looked around and realized exactly what it was I was seeing. Tobacco residue. Someone had been chopping up tobacco to place in some of the food.

Why would someone put tobacco in bakery items, I wondered, and then I had a flashback to my doctor's appointments. They had found nicotine in my system. Not only that, but the oxygen level in my blood had been low – a side effect of... of chloroform.

But, I hadn't eaten any brownies at the party,

In fact, the oxygen thing had been a problem for a couple of weeks, but I had assumed it was from the incident a month ago when I had been exposed to carbon monoxide.

My breath hitched. It was all right there in front of me. Cassandra had been making me my own batches of brownies for weeks – filling it with traces of chloroform and plenty of nicotine.

She had been slowly poisoning me and getting me addicted to her brownies! No wonder I had eaten a whole plate of those one night!

But, she must have gotten impatient. I thought back to the video; she had totally doused that one batch – instead of trying to poison me slowly, she decided to try to take me out at the after party!

And, she hired me as her private investigator to throw me – and probably the police – off her trail! The whole time I had been thinking that Morgan or Cassandra had been the victim, but it had been me!

No wonder I didn't like that brownie at the party; it'd been the wrong type of brownie and had just been coated in the icing that I liked!

I snapped a picture of the tobacco box, thinking maybe Deb might need it. I knew Cassandra was my client, but it was clear now that that had all been a ruse. She was the true culprit!

I spun around, and there she was.

Cassandra.

"Kate, what are you doing back here?" she asked innocently.

"Just seeing if I can find anything for the case," I said. "So far, nothing."

My heart raced. Laurie was here.

"Nothing?" she asked, and glared at me.

I suddenly recalled the feeling of being watched in my own house. It'd been Cassandra!

Now, her eyes fell toward my right hand where I was holding my phone. "What did you just take a picture of?" she asked.

We stared at each other, and I think she knew.

She was busted. Her little plan had failed. And, I was ticked. She was trying to kill me so that she could get with Jim! Not only had she been flirting with my husband, sending him naked pictures, and calling the police on him to make him look like the guilty party – but she'd been trying to kill me and my babies! My pregnancy was at risk because of this psychopath.

And she'd made me doubt my darling devoted husband.

Cassandra stepped toward me, but I darted out of her way and into the front of the shop.

"It's Cassandra!" I shouted at Deb who was still sitting and feeding Laurie bits of muffin. "And, don't feed Laurie anything from here!"

My shouts were not much of an explanation, but I suppose the freaked out look on my face was enough to get Deb up and moving. I've never seen anyone whip a kid out of a high chair so quick. As Deb was placing Laurie on her hip, Cassandra came bursting out of the kitchen wielding a kitchen knife.

"Duck!" Deb shouted at me, and I obeyed quickly. I'm glad I did because Deb's half empty cup of hot coffee went flinging over my head and straight into Cassandra's face. The thing busted against her forehead before sending her flying onto her back.

"Whoa!" I yelped. "What an arm!"

Cassandra scrambled to her feet again. With the adrenaline pumping through my system, I kicked at her arm, using one of my kick-boxing maneuvers and knocked the knife out of her hand.

"Get Laurie out of here!" I shrieked, but it didn't look like Deb – a cop – had any interest in leaving me alone with someone as loopy as Cassandra.

Cassandra, her face bloodied, held out her hands like they were claws. I wasn't in the mood for a cat fight, but it looked like she sure was. She ran at me, grabbing my hair and punching at my belly.

I swiveled out of her grasp and punched her nose.

She yelped, but then suddenly flew backward through the air and landed on the floor.

I gasped. I knew my punch hadn't flung her back like that.

A figure emerged and I realized it was Jim, eyes blazing. He blocked me from Cassandra and looked ready to murder her.

"All right, easy there, big guy," Deb said, plopping Laurie into my arms. She immediately pressed her knee into Cassandra's spine to immobilize her. "Shoot, I don't have my cuffs," Deb groaned. "Looks like I'm just going to have to sit on you until a uniformed officer gets here."

"I told you she was crazy!" Jim snapped. "Did she attack you? What happened?"

"Cassandra killed Morgan," I said, deciding not to give him the detail that I was the intended victim just yet. I'd wait until Cassandra was in the back of a cop car so Jim didn't have the opportunity to go after her again.

Deb called in backup around the time Trixie wandered back inside from a smoke break. The woman looked very confused, and Cassandra just cussed when she questioned what was going on.

"Yeah, you might want to keep your mouth shut," Deb warned, placing a hand on the back of Cassandra's head and making her kiss the floor. "You tried to sock my girl in her gut. Not cool," Deb said, winking up at me. She held out a hand toward Jim. "Deb, by the way. You must be Jim."

Jim shook his head. "Yeah, nice to meet you..." he said, shaking her hand, but then he laughed slightly as he looked down at Deb who was so casual about detaining a very frantic woman.

Backup arrived at last, and Deb spoke with the officer as he placed a cuffed Cassandra into the back of his patrol car. Deb was sober enough now to give her statement without letting the other officer realize she'd been drinking only a few hours earlier. "You mind coming in early so you can see your perp down to the station?" the officer asked.

"Actually, I think I need to go home and shower," Deb said. "I'll be there soon, though. Promise." Deb then motioned in my direction. "We need to see what we can do for this girl. She solved this case for us."

The officer agreed, shook my hand, and was about to drive off. I couldn't help but to throw a snide comment Cassandra's way. "I'll bill you for the case," I said.

Cassandra smirked angrily at me from the other side of the car window.

"What, you're not going to pay me now?" I questioned, and she looked away.

Jim placed a hand on my shoulder. "Are you all right, baby?"

I smiled at him. "I am now."

CHAPTER 17

*I*t was closing night of the play, and of course, I had come out to attend along with Jim and Paula and even Deb. We all sat together, shaking our heads at the disaster of a comedy/musical once more. Although, I have to say, now that I knew what to expect I enjoyed the play much more. There was going to be another after party for closing night – this time the director made the food for it himself.

No more chances, I guess.

After the play, the audience trickled out, and the cast and crew made their way to the lobby for the after party. The food wasn't quite as elegant as it had been opening night, but the director was far too nervous to order food again. Fried chicken, refried beans, and rice. Honestly, it was a pregnant woman's dream. "I can't believe you're eating food here," Jim teased.

"I'm pregnant, and this is fried chicken," I said. "Yeah, I'm eating."

"How is your pregnancy going thus far?" Paula asked as Deb sat down with me to gobble up some food as well.

"A lot better now that I'm not slowly ingesting nicotine and chloroform," I said.

"Yeah, that'll do it," Paula said, shaking her head. "Is what Cassandra did to you going to hurt the babies?"

I frowned. I really didn't want to think about that. "Right now, everything is checking out okay. But, between the carbon monoxide poisoning last month, the high dosage of nicotine, and the chloroform, my doctor is keeping a very close eye on me. But, two healthy heart beats, and they have started to wiggle a little. It took me forever to start to feel Laurie moving around in there, but I started feeling these two pretty quickly."

"Second pregnancy," Paula said. "With my second I noticed it way earlier. They say it's because you know what you're expecting or something like that. So, you don't mistake it for indigestion or whatever."

Jim sat down, a very empty looking plate in front of him. He'd been a nervous wreck over the past several days, so he had been eating like a bird. I smiled at him, and he smiled back. He was worried about the babies after I had given him the rundown on everything that Cassandra had done. I think a part of him blamed himself; he had been the one running off to get me those poisoned brownies every couple of days.

But how was he supposed to know she'd doused them with nicotine and poison to attempt to slowly kill me? Frankly, the one and only reason we caught her is because she had gotten impatient and had tried to finish me off at the party.

The scary part was, if those brownies hadn't gotten mixed up, I probably would have eaten several of the poisoned ones. But, I had bit into a different brownies recipe that had merely been disguised as one of my tasty purple brownie treats. Thank goodness because she had put enough chloroform in there to kill someone who hadn't already been being regularly poisoned by her.

Mom came trotting up, having changed out of her costume, and she plopped down at the little table where the rest of us were seated. "Well, this was a fun little adventure," she said, glancing up and waving Galigani over who had gotten lost in the crowd.

"What, the play, or Kate's case?" Deb asked.

"Both," my mom said. "Not sure if acting is for me."

I laughed. Knowing Mom, she was ready to for her next big adventure. We all chatted about the play and the case – Deb enjoyed giving Jim a hard time about Cassandra stalking him.

He wasn't a fan of her poking fun, but he went along with it anyway. He was a sensitive man, but he could take a few jokes. I was so glad that we were going to be able to put this whole Cassandra thing behind us, and I was especially glad that we had gathered up enough evidence to convict her.

According to Deb, she was going to be spending a lot of time behind bars for this one. There was something oddly satisfying about knowing your husband's ex-girlfriend was going to be hanging out in a jail cell for an extended vacation.

As we were all laughing and having a good time, I spotted Domingo sulking in a corner and drowning his sorrows in soda and fried chicken. He and I had had our differences, but I can't imagine what it must feel like to have something you worked so hard on and put so much of yourself into become the local laughing stock.

I excused myself from my friends and family for a moment and wandered over to Domingo, plopping myself down in the empty seat beside him.

"No amount of fried chicken is going to make you feel better," I teased lightly, and he sat back and wiped his face and hands on a napkin before chugging a bit of his soda to wash the crumbly meal down.

"No, probably not," he said, shaking his head as he sat his soda down. "You come over here to poke fun at me?"

"No, that sounds more like something you would do," I said, crossing my arms. "You know, I've read the original script. And, as much as it pains me to say it, you're an excellent writer, Domingo. I just wish your play had gotten into the right director's hands. One who wouldn't have rewritten half the play just to get a few laughs... or added in a random musical number."

"Yeah, that one hurt," Domingo admitted, but he laughed slightly. "It... it was kind of funny, I guess."

"Oh, no, it was hilarious. Very slapstick, but I still like your version of it a lot better," I said, and the man broke into a slight smile. I sat upright. "Did *you* just smile at me?"

It was immediately gone; he broke into a scowl. "Well, don't get used to it. And, thank you, Kate. I appreciate hearing that."

"Maybe you can find another director willing to put on the show?" I suggested.

"People will expect to see a comedy now," he said. "This was the show's debut, and it got a decent amount of attention. Now, people are going to expect it to be funny. If I go to some other playhouse and put this thing on, the audience will buy tickets expecting to see a comedy. That twerp ruined this for me."

"Sorry, Vicente," I said.

We sat together in silence for a moment and then he said, "Kate, I'm proud of you. You did a great job cracking this case. You've really got gusto." He stood and walked off, depositing his half-eaten dinner in a trash bin.

Was that a compliment?

Yeah, I decided it was. I headed back to my group of friends, but by now the party was starting to die down. "I say we go back to Jim and Kate's place and make margaritas," Deb said.

"Well, look at that," Deb said with a wink. "Come on, my treat. I'll pick up the ingredients on the way. I know you have that fancy blender."

Jim leaned over and whispered to me, "Has this woman been in our house?" I just shrugged, knowing that my friendship with Deb was going to be very interesting.

Jim laughed and smiled. "You know what? I could use a margarita."

"Hazzah!" Deb exclaimed. "This is my type of guy right here, well, if I had a type of that sort."

The End

OTHER TITLES BY DIANA ORGAIN

ABOUT THE AUTHOR

Diana Orgain is the *USA Today* Bestselling author of the MATERNAL INSTINCTS MYSTERY SERIES, the iWITCH MYSTERY SERIES and the GLUTEN-FREE MYSTERY SERIES. She is the co-author of NY Times Bestselling *Scrapbooking Mystery Series* with Laura Childs. Diana's FOR LOVE OR MONEY SERIES is now available as is her ROUNDUP CREW MYSTERY SERIES: *Yappy Hour* and *Trigger Yappy*. For a complete listing of books, as well as excerpts and contests, and to connect with Diana:

Visit Diana's website at www.dianaorgain.com.